AGM2

A New York State Of Mind

Sean A Wright

ACKNOWLEDGEMENTS

First and foremost I want to thank Almighty God, for blessing me with the gift of writing, followed by the gift of success. Without you God, none of this would be possible. I am forever grateful.

To my parents Janice and Larry Wright: How ironic is it that moms last name is Reid and Dads last name is Wright. I guess this is what I was destined to do huh? Your combined guidance is what made me the man that I am today. I love you both. Thank you.

To my brothers and sister, nieces and nephews: I love you all unconditionally.

To my kids Michael and Daisy: Remember, you have to do what you got to do, so you can do what you want to do! I love you both!

To my partner Fred Lee: Just the other day you said to me; "We are blessed, not everybody can do it like us." As long as I have known you that has got to be one of the realest things you have ever said. (well that and the time you admitted that the Cowboys need to get rid of Tony Romo...lol) We did it again my G!! Now let's get to this Corporate money.

To my self-adpoted parents Deb and Fred Lee: Thank you for always making me feel welcomed in your home. I greatly appreciate the continued support from both of you.

To Theresa Henderson: Thank you for doing my cover and my video. You did your thing.

To Junnita Jackson: Thank you so much for another smash cover.

To Chelly: I have no problem saying that there is absolutely no way this project would have been completed without your diligence and hard work. Without your help I honestly don't know what stage of AGM2 I would be at right now. Thanks for putting up with my indecisiveness, and for cracking the with whip when procrastination often started to set in. I can honestly and truly say you are heaven sent. Take a bow Chelly, this victory is just as much yours as it is mines. You are greatly appreciated. #LFB

To Jah Channer: Thanks for "Shaking" The stick and keeping me on my toes. "BIG UP"...lol

To Team Sean Wright: Thank you for taking time out of your busy schedules to keep my name relevant during my hiatus to finish AGM2.

To all of the Bloggers, Radio Stations, and Magazines: Thank you for taking the time to spotlight me as a relevant new author in the game.

To My Urban Book Club, Real Readers & Authors R Us, Black E-Book Club, Black Faithful Sisters & Brothers, Nook Readers, We Read Urban Fiction: Thank you for all of your continued support.

To my Silverback Crew: AGM Double!!!! I got crazy love for all of you. Thanks for the support.

AND FINALLY TO ALL OF MY LOYAL SUPPORTERS WHO SUPPORTED ME AND KEPT PUSHING FOR THE RELEASE OF AGM 2: YOU ARE ALL SO VERY MUCH APPRECIATED. I SAY IT ALL THE TIME ON FACEBOOK "WITHOUT YOU, THERE IS NO ME!"

A GANGSTER'S MELODY 2
A NEW YORK STATE OF MIND

PROLOGUE

I woke up and rolled over to see my baby Travon sleeping peacefully after a long night of making love to me. I leaned over and kissed him on the cheek.

"Good morning baby."

He rolled over and kissed me back with his morning breath, but I didn't even mind.

"Tiffany you're the greatest baby. Who would have ever thought we would have made it through all of that bullshit?" he asked talking to me with his eyes still closed.

"Yeah well you lucky I understand why you did what you did and I love you so much that I can put that all behind us," I said lying across his chest as he played in my hair.

"You know we're gonna have to leave town and never look back right?" he mumbled still not opening his eyes.

"What about your wife and kids?"

"They'll be well provided for, but I can never go back to them. They're just gonna have to take it on the chin."

"What do you mean they're gonna have to take it on the chin?" I replied, disturbed by his remarks.

"Tiffany, when my wife got involved with me she knew exactly what she was getting into. She knew my lifestyle and she knew the risk and everything that was involved."

"And your kids?"

"Collateral damage. Like I said, they will be well provided for," he answered just as cold as a Christmas day in Manhattan.

I couldn't believe my ears. Is this what he felt about us losing *our* baby? Was our baby just collateral damage? Was I supposed to charge everything he put me through to the game? I could feel my eyes watering as my bottom lip started to quiver. I could tell by Travon's heavy breathing that he had fallen back asleep. I eased my head up off of his chest as I replayed his words over and over again in my mind. The words were like a soundtrack to the mental movie that was being played in my head. Visions of our first kiss, our first night together, Monica and the girls, my parents, my grandmother, the money, the cars, the houses, the fame, the fortune, the trips, the salons, the cops, the handcuffs, the lies, the set up, the courthouse, the bullshit testimony, the death of my baby and the jail cell doors closing. It was then that I was once again overcome with grief and as the tears silently flooded my face, and it was then that I decided that love or no love, he should not be able to dictate the outcome of people's lives and hurt them at will. I would make sure that it would never happen again. I grabbed the Desert Eagle that he left laying on the nightstand. I chambered a round

2

and took it off safety. I straddled his chest then nudged him slightly and quietly called his name to wake him up. When he opened his eyes, he was staring down the barrel of his own gun. I'm sure he wanted to know what was going on, but if the thoughts were going to reach his brain, they would have to take a detour through the pillows and the sheets as I spat in his face and squeezed the trigger… I jumped up from my sleep, stared at the bars in my jail cell and turned over to make an attempt at getting back to sleep.

JAIL BAIT

I was awakened by the sound of Michelle moaning and groaning from playing with herself. I jumped down off my bunk and kneeled down beside her. She was so lost in her own world; with her eyes closed and rolled up into her damn head, that she didn't even notice me. I watched for a moment as she used one hand to rub on her clit and the other to massage her breasts. She was breathing heavily so whomever she was fucking in her fantasy was apparently doing a good job. She then proceeded to insert two fingers inside herself and moved them in and out in rapid succession as her panting got deeper and heavier. She licked her lips and bit down on the bottom one never opening her eyes. The moans got louder, her fingers went deeper, and her legs began to shake slightly and that's when I knew she was about to reach her climax, but it would never happen. I waited until she was almost there and slapped her viciously across the face awakening her from her fantasy and bring her back to reality.

"Bitch I thought we already spoke about this?" I spat as she awakened from her trance.

"Tiffany baby I'm sorry, I was dreaming. I didn't mean anything by it."

I grabbed her by her face.

"You thinking about that nigga Bobby again ain't you? That sorry ass motherfucker who ain't sent your ass a dime the whole time you been in here. Who has been holding you down for the past eighteen months?"

"You have Tiffany, but you're hurting me baby."

"Shut the fuck up and assume the position, before shit really get funky up in here," I barked as I released her face and she slowly got out of her bunk and dropped to her knees.

As I stood in front of her, I dropped my panties, grabbed her head, and force-fed her my pussy. I wasn't even in the mood for no head, but I wasn't going to be disrespected. Not after Travon, never again. Those who know me or should I say those that knew me, know that the old Tiffany wasn't even into this lesbian shit, but that's what a three hundred and seventy two year sentence will do to you. All this violence and aggression day in and day out is what a no good nigga and a failed system did to me. So the goody two shoes, square ass Tiffany died along with my unborn baby in that courtroom four years ago. This is the new me, this is the me that *they* created and I was getting used to it.

✳✳✳✳✳

"Davis you got a package," I could hear C.O. Washington yell as she made her way down the tier. I got down off my bunk and stood at the door of my cell as she approached with my package and mail.

"Girl, I am so tired of delivering these damn packages to you. You might as well make me your personal mail service," she joked as she passed me the items.

"Thanks Washington, you cute and all but I'm in need of a different type of male service if you know what I mean?" I responded.

"Mmm mmm mmm Tiff you are something else. I tell you what though; I gotta admire you for keeping your head up and being able to joke with all that you have been through. I honestly don't know how you do it."

"Shit, it's a struggle every day but with God and my girl Monica holding me down all this time, it definitely makes it easier."

"Well I'll tell you what, you are one of the very few people in here that I believe is innocent and everyone else who followed your story on the news believes it too."

"Yeah, I appreciate it, but twelve jurors and a judge didn't believe me and at this point that's all that matters. But hey, it's all good. You live and you learn," I said fighting back a tear that was trying to kick box its way out of my left eye.

"Yo C.O. hurry up with the fuckin' mail," an inmate shouted from across the tier.

"Oh shut the hell up Pumpkin, you don't ever get shit anyway," Washington spat back.

"Girl let me go before they complain about us fraternizing."

"Okay Washington, thanks again for the pep talk."

"Anytime girl. You know we gotta stick together," she responded as she continued down the tier on her mail run.

I was cool with the majority of the C.O.'s but Washington and I were really close, probably because we came to Cumberland Federal Prison on the same day, obviously me as an inmate and her as an officer. Her first duty that day was to break up a fight in the shower between me and some chick who thought just because she was way bigger than me that she was going to take my jailhouse virginity. I admit, she whooped my ass but it wasn't easy and I kept my jailhouse virginity. Washington had her escorted to the hole and she escorted me to the infirmary. On the way there she told me that she had recognized me from various newspaper articles and mentioned that there were tons of women out in the world that had my back and believed in my innocence. We have been cool ever since.

I didn't even look to see who the package was from. I already knew it was from Monica. She was the only one who sent me packages. Most of the mail was pity letters from people who followed my case and the daily letter from that ole' bitch who still has the audacity to call herself my Grandmother. I made sure every fucking letter she sent me was thrown away unopened. After what she did to me in the courtroom that day, the only thing she could do for me is drop dead. Monica's packages and mail came faithfully and she hardly ever missed a visit. I unfolded the flaps on the already opened package to see that Monica had come through for me once again. I had my Japanese cherry blossom products, my feminine hygiene stuff, some Vicky

Secrets boy shorts and bras, some mix CD's, and most importantly the newest book releases from my favorite author Sean A. Wright. Some of this was considered contraband but they do things a little different here in the Feds. Since they always open the package before it gets to me, they would always take the stuff they wanted and keep it for themselves, so Monica started putting more than enough in there for the C.O.'s and me. I unfolded a small note that Monica sent along with the care package.

"Here you go you spoiled bitch. You be costing me a grip, but it's all good. You're Grandmother asked about you again when I stopped by the house to pick up the rent from my tenants. I know you told me to tell her to rot in hell but Tiff, she's still ya family and you should at least hear what she has to say. We all we got left. See you in a few days."

Monica was right. We were all we had left. Terri was dead and her murder was still unsolved, I was gonna be in jail for the next six million years for a crime I didn't commit, and Lashawn found God, denounced the street life, and moved to Arizona with some guy she met on www.christianlove.com. So Monica was all alone on the streets. The Stiletto Diva's as we knew them were no more. I asked Monica why she just didn't recruit new girls, and she simply replied that we could not be replaced and I guess she was right. We had a bond, we had history, we had triumph and we had tragedy. As for my Grandmother, as far as I'm concerned, she was a non-factor in my life before I got to Baltimore, as well as during the short time I was forced to live with her and that nasty ass old man that looked like a reformed pedophile. There is nothing she could ever say to me to make me forgive her for fuckin' me over in the courtroom that day.

Michelle coming into the cell interrupted my thoughts. She had been sent here eighteen months ago for credit card fraud and identity theft. She was getting bread with her sorry ass man Bobby, but as soon as shit hit the fan he got ghost and left her holding the bag. When Michelle got here, she was just like me, shy, timid and afraid. She had no family, she put her life in the hands of a nigga that she thought loved her and just like me she was wrong. It's sad because Michelle is beautiful. She's 5'7, dark chocolate complexion, slanted eyes, beautiful smile and her body is stacked. When they made her my celly, I told her I would look out for her just like my old head Pam had looked out for me when I first got here, before she died from somebody putting ground glass in her oatmeal. In any event, I showed Michelle the ropes and we got along great and it would be her that I lost my jailhouse virginity to, but she wouldn't take it, I would give it to her willingly. Ironically it would be her that was awakened by *my* moaning and groaning from my self-administered sexual pleasures. This night, she would watch me as my eyes were closed, but she didn't stop me. Instead she pleasured herself while she watched. I had no idea I had become her personal porn movie until she let out an uncontrollable moan. I jumped up, but for some reason I wasn't angry or embarrassed. Instead I climbed down off my bunk, pulled her close to me and gently began kissing her. She offered no resistance as we made passionate love on the cell floor. From that moment on she was my sex toy and jailhouse bitch. She would do as she was told no questions asked. If she followed suit she would reap the benefits, if she refused to toe the line, then there would be consequences, hence last night's incident.

"Hey baby. I bought you back a turkey and cheese from the mess hall. I snuck it out after I cleaned up," she said with a smile on her face.

"That's what's up. Did you make it just the way I like it?" I asked not looking up from my package.

"Of course I did baby. I put pickles and chips on the side too. "

"Aww. Ain't you sweet? Put it on the shelf and I will bust it down as soon as I finish going through this package."

"Damn Tiff, you stay with a fuckin' package. It must be nice."

"Oh shut up. I always share with you so stop ya crying," I joked.

"That's because you love me and you know I love you back," she responded attempting to hug me as I pushed her off.

"Bitch please. Don't nobody love you and you don't love me. What the fuck I tell you about that word?"

"Love nobody but yourself," she answered sadly.

"Alright then. Let that be the last time I hear them words come out ya mouth."

On Friday morning when they cracked the cells I felt like a kid on Christmas. It was visiting day and I knew Monica would be there like clockwork. After my daily routine of working out, chow hall, and working in the library, I waited patiently for the clock to hit 2pm so I could see my homie, and then right on schedule I heard the C.O. yell.

"Davis, you got a visitor."

I gave myself the once over and hurried to the visiting area where Monica sat patiently waiting.

"What's up girl?" I said as I gave Monica a brief hug per the prison rules.

"Hey bitch, what's popping?" she replied returning the hug and kissed me on the cheek.

"Well it definitely ain't my lip gloss now-a-days," I joked.

"Bitch you silly," Monica responded as we shared a laugh and sat down.

"So what's new?" I asked as if whatever was new would have any effect on me.

"Well you know ya Grandmother still harassing me about bringing her tired ass up here to see you, but I already let her know that you ain't trying to hear nothing she got to say. Seriously though Tiff, she ain't looking too good. Other than that, ain't shit else. Motherfuckers still dying, going to jail left and right, and in between doing that, I'm still taking them for everything they got."

"Some things never change. Girl you a trip, but I feel you, fuck 'em all, including that old bitch."

"You already know, but damn Tiff, you seriously don't give a fuck about ya peoples huh? I don't blame you so I ain't gonna stress you about it no more. So how you holding up?"

"The best way I can. I'm still waiting on a miracle. I keep praying, but when the feds seized my money and assets, my lawyer quit on me and the public defender ain't really doing shit."

"It's cool girl, something gotta give. I don't even know why you sitting in this shit hole. I mean everybody know this case is bogus as fuck."

"Yeah tell me about it, but because the case is so high profile, no judge wants to review it again."

"Look Ma, everybody ain't gonna keep shitting on you, somebody's gonna cave in."

"Yeah well I hope so. This jail shit is getting too easy."

"Well that's a good thing right?"

"Hell no. That means I'm getting comfortable. I gotta get the fuck outta here."

PILLOW TALK

I was in my cell waiting for Michelle to bring my lunch from the chow hall, when Sheila ran up rambling and out of breath.

"A yo Tiff. You better come quick."

"What the hell is wrong with you? What happened?"

"Marsha and Ashley ran up on your girl Michelle in the dayroom. They giving her the business right now."

Marsha was the bitch who they say put the ground glass in my old head Pam's oatmeal. She started running shit in the prison after Pam died, but she didn't run it like Pam. Pam ran the prison off of her respect. Marsha thrived on running it off of fear. Those that feared her, buckled at her request. Those who didn't did just as I was about to do, take it straight to that bitch. I jumped up, quickly grabbed an empty pillowcase, stuffed it with nine or ten bars of soap and ran down the tier towards the day room. When I got there, that bitch Corporal Ruiz was standing guard outside the door. I could hear the commotion going on inside and was ready for war. There were a lot of crooked C.O.'s at Cumberland, but Ruiz was one of the dirtiest. She and I had problems in the past, so I knew this was going to be a task.

"Keep it moving Davis," she said with her arms folded.

"Get the fuck out of my way Ruiz."

"Go on about your business Davis. I'm warning you."

I wound the pillowcase around my fist.

"Look. Either you let me in, or I start with you."

She chuckled slightly.

"You know what you little mouthy bitch. I'm going to go ahead and let you in there and I hope Big Marsha and Ashley wear your little ass out and fuck you good after."

I pushed passed her and entered the dayroom where Marsha and Ashley were pushing Michelle back and forth and slapping her around. Each time she tried to fight back, they gave it to her worse. I had seen enough.

"Back the fuck up off her Marsha."

"Mind your business Tiffany. This ain't got shit to do with you," she replied.

"When it involves my celly, it has everything to do with me."

"Well you got two choices. You can pay her debt of twenty-two cartons of cigarettes, or you can join her in this ass whooping. If you're really lucky, I'll lick your wounds when I'm done."

"Look Marsha, I know the rules. If she got a debt with you, then she needs to make good and she will. Just give her some time."

"This bitch done had enough time. Now I gave you two choices."

"Well I don't smoke, so I guess we're going to have to rock out," I said as I approached with my pillowcase gripped tightly in my hand.

"Look why don't you take your laundry and get the fuck..."

She never got a chance to finish her sentence because I took my soap filled pillowcase and knocked it back down her throat. The first blow shattered her teeth instantly, splattering blood everywhere. I then instinctively swung around and caught her cohort Ashley in the face breaking her nose and knocking her unconscious. I turned my attention back to Marsha who was screaming in pain while Michelle punched and kicked her viciously. I grabbed Michelle to stop her.

"Now Marsha I'm going to ask you again. Can Michelle have a little more time to pay you what she owes?"

"Yeah, she can have a week, but you won't be around to see it. You'll be dead by the end of the night bitch," she said looking up from the floor.

"Damn. I hate being threatened," I replied as I swung my pillowcase with all my might hitting her in the mid section, knocking the wind out of her as Michelle spat in her face and we headed out of the dayroom.

Once we were out of the dayroom, Corporal Ruiz looked in, saw what we had done and immediately blew her code red whistle. Her backup arrived in seconds and Michelle and I were whisked away to the hole. After just a few hours in the hole, I could hear Michelle losing her mind.

"Somebody please, please help me. Let me out of here," she screamed.

"Hey Michelle," I yelled out.

"Tiffany, help me. It's dark, I can't see and there are things crawling all over me," she cried out.

"Michelle calm down. Breathe. There is nothing crawling on you. It's all in your mind," I yelled back.

"No it's not. They're biting me Tiffany. They're all over me. Somebody help me please."

Other inmates in the hole were laughing hysterically and making a mockery of Michelle.

"Listen at the new booty crying like a little bitch," one inmate yelled out.

"If I come and help you then you belong to me and that pussy is mines," another one continued.

"Ya'll bitches shut the fuck up. Michelle don't listen to them hoes. Focus on my voice and my voice only. Everything is going to be okay," I said trying to sound reassuring.

This went on for an hour, maybe more, until I could no longer hear Michelle. I called out her name repeatedly but got no answer. I prayed to God that she was okay.

My prayers were answered the next morning, when Michelle and I were escorted to the warden's office to answer for the melee' in the dayroom.

"Davis and Henderson, can either of you tell me why I have two inmates in the infirmary? One has a concussion and a broken nose, and the other has a fractured jaw and needs reconstructive oral surgery," he stated.

"Sir, it was strictly self defense, but if any additional punishment needs to be handed down, then I want to go on record by saying that Michelle had nothing to do with this. I caused all of the injuries, and I am willing to take whatever punishment comes my way," I said looking him dead in the eye.

"All by yourself huh? Henderson is this true?"

"No Sir we both…."

"I acted alone sir. Michelle is just trying to be a good celly," I interjected.

"Well in any event, it's only because both of you have kept your noses clean while Marsha and Ashley have had such a bad track record that I'm going to go easy on you. Davis you have two weeks with no phone or visiting privileges. Henderson, because Davis is willing to take the blame for it all you get off scott free this time, but I'm warning you both. If either of you are brought before me again, it won't be pretty."

"Yes Sir," we both said in unison.

"Good. Guard take them back to their cells."

As we were lead back to our cell. Michelle grabbed my hand.

"Thanks Tiff."

"It ain't about shit, but from here on out the next time you have a debt you damn well better be able to cover it."

"I got you."

BLOOD THINNER

From the moment I stepped foot inside Cumberland Federal Prison, Monica had been trying to get me to patch things up with my dad's mother. I had vehemently declined all visit requests and returned her letters but today would be different. Today I would attempt to put my bitterness aside. During Monica's last visit, she told me that my dad's mother was sick. She had been sick for years, but this time was different. Monica said that she was frequently being carted off to the hospital by an ambulance. Monica also said she looked really bad and could barely walk on her own. Apparently her days were really numbered. I knew my dad would want me to see her as one of her final wishes, so I finally put her on the visitors list and allowed Monica to bring her up to see me today. The crazy thing was that out of all the time I had been locked up, this was one visit I was not looking forward to.

When I was called for my visit, for the first time ever, I walked slow towards the visiting room hoping that the travel time would eat up a good portion of the visit. As I approached the visiting room, I saw Monica looking sharp as every from her hair down to her feet. My dad's mom on the other hand looked like death ten times over. She looked frail, brittle and she had lost a lot of weight. She was toting around a portable oxygen tank, and despite all the hell that she put me through I could not help but to feel sorry for her. As I approached the table Monica jumped up quickly hugging me in usual fashion. Meanwhile Lula Belle couldn't even look me in my face.

"Hey Tiff. Girl you getting a little thick ain't you?"

"Oh whatever, I still look good, don't be hating."

"Oh trust me, ain't nobody hating boo. You might have a better body, but I pull better niggas."

"Shit that's what you think. In my mind I go to sleep with Denzel every night."

We both shared a quick laugh.

"So ya'll just gonna keep talking like I ain't sitting here?" Mama Belle said as if each word might take her last breath.

"Hi Lula Belle," I said rolling my eyes and sitting down.

"Since when do you address your grandmother by her first name child?" she mustered up the strength to say.

"My grandmother? Really? Come on Lula Belle. Are we going to start the visit off on the wrong foot?"

"Tiffany I ain't been nothing but good to you from the time you stepped off that damn Greyhound. I took you in, found you a job and tried my best to love you."

I had heard enough already.

"Love me? Love me? You're part of the reason why I'm sitting in this motherfucker. You damn near forced me into Travon's arms, and if that wasn't enough, you get on the stand and say you knew I was into some shady shit? You were the only family I had. Your testimony could have saved my life, but instead you put the fucking nail in my coffin."

"Tiffany what did you expect me to say? I reported what I saw. I didn't lie. Everything I said was true. The money, the houses, the fancy cars, all of that was real. I didn't make any of it up."

"You know damn well I wasn't no motherfucking drug kingpin. You knew I was just a victim of circumstance and you didn't lift a finger to save me. As my walls crumbled around me, you sat back and watched. All because of some dumb ass beef you had with my mom, who by the way spoke very highly of you while she was alive."

"Tiffany I didn't know you. I had no idea where there the money was coming from. How was I supposed to know that you were innocent?"

"If nothing else you should have been confident in the way that your son raised me."

"Well how was I supposed to know how he raised you?"

"Because you raised him," I snapped.

I had stuck her with that last remark and she had no real comeback. I was crying from rage and anger as this dumb ass debate re-opened wounds that I wanted to keep closed. My blood was boiling and I didn't know how much longer I could sit here and take this shit, however there was one question that had been burning my soul for years now.

"Lula Belle let me ask you a question. If you suspected that the money was dirty and obtained by ill gotten means, why the hell didn't you return any of those checks I was sending you before I got booked?"

"Because I needed the money Tiffany. Social Security only takes me but so far, then I'm scraping for the remainder of the month, Rufus drinks up his money, so those checks were coming right on time."

Did this old bitch just say what I think she said?

"Sooo let me get this right? You told the prosecutor that my money was dirty, yet you spent every fucking dime that I sent you without even so much as a call to say thank you."

"Why would I call you Tiffany? We weren't even speaking to each other?"

"Wow. Really? Okay I'm done," I said as I started to get up from the table.

"Haven't you gotten any of my letters? I've sent dozens. "

"Yup and I threw all them shits away unopened. Good bye Lula Belle."

"Tiffany wait, I need money. I need lots of money. They are about to foreclose on my house and I need operations that Medicare won't cover. Tiffany you are all that I got," she pleaded as Monica and I just sat there with our mouths hanging open at her audacity.

"Are you out of your fucking mind? First of all, don't you see me doing about nine life sentences in this motherfucker, second of all, if I wasn't locked up what makes you think I would give you another fucking dime, and where would I get it from anyway?" I snapped

"Now come on Tiffany, I know you still got some of that drug money tucked away somewhere. It ain't doing you no good in here, let grandmama have it and put it to good use."

I couldn't believe my ears, my temperature immediately shot up to one hundred and five as I got up from the table.

"You know what you old bitch. If we wasn't on the first floor, I'd roll your trifling ass down the steps. Monica get this bitch out of my sight. She is officially dead to me, and if you ever mention her name to me again, you'll be dead to me too," I barked.

"Tiffany wait, I need your help I'm going to die baby," she pleaded.

"Well tell Mama and Daddy I said hi then."

"Monica talk to her. Tell her to help me. She listens to you. Make her help her grandmother."

"Sorry Ms. Belle, you are totally out of pocket. Now I'm going to help you get home, but after that, don't contact me again. I'm through with you too," Monica said helping her to her feet.

"See you next week Monica," I said as I stormed off.

Three weeks later, Monica wrote me and told me my father's mother had died. So even if I had the money to help that bitch get medical treatment, she would have died any damn way. As much as I wanted to feel some remorse about losing a blood relative, I just couldn't find it in me to shed one tear.

CHANGE GONE' COME

Over the next few months, my daily life as an inmate continued as usual. With each day that passed, I became more comfortable and acclimated to the fact that I was a prisoner and that I would die a prisoner, still with each visit from Monica I wanted to be free. I was starting to believe that would never happen, until one Saturday I was in the dayroom playing spades when C.O. Jefferies came in.

"Davis you got a visitor."

"On a Saturday?" I asked a little perplexed because only attorneys were allowed to visit on off days, and I had just saw my sorry as lawyer two days ago and he had no new info for me.

"Look, don't question it. Just hurry up before I shut it down," she said nastily.

I rolled my eyes, told the girls I would be back and proceeded to be escorted down to the visiting room for this surprise visit. About halfway there Jefferies broke the silence.

"So Davis, who's responsible for Deanna getting her face cut yesterday?"

I stopped dead in my tracks.

"Oh is that what this was about? I should have known something was up. I ain't see shit, I ain't hear shit and I don't know shit, so you might as well take me back to the dayroom," I said sharply, lying through my teeth.

"Keep walking. This has nothing to do with that," she instructed.

As we approached the visiting room, It was completely empty with the exception of a young black woman in a navy blue business pantsuit, with some nice ass shoes and a brief case. Jefferies opened the door to allow me to enter, and then she advised the mystery woman that she would be right outside as she closed the door.

"Ms. Davis, please have a seat," she instructed.

I sat down and popped the question.

"Who are you and what is this about?" I asked a little defensively.

"My name is Sophia Garrison and I'm an attorney out of New York City. Tiffany, I traveled all this way because I believe I have some information that could very well result in an overturn of your conviction."

My mouth dropped wide open and the words "Look bitch, I ain't in the mood for no games," accidentally forced their way outta of my mouth.

"Ms. Davis, I can assure you that this is no game. The truth of the matter is I have been following your case since it started and when you were convicted I started using all of my free time to fill in the holes that this case seems to be so full of."

"Keep talking, I'm listening," I said excitedly.

"Well apparently, Travon's associate Darren Barnes kept extensive records on the crews activity."

"There must be some mistake. I don't know a Darren Barns."

"You may know him as D-Boy. It's believed that Travon may have executed him outside of the courthouse the day you were convicted."

"Yeah, I heard about that. And that bastard is still walking around freely huh," I snapped now getting agitated.

"Well hopefully not for long. It appears that the new owners of Darren's house were doing some re-modeling and found some sort of secret stash spot in the house. Apparently he kept detailed memoirs of all the crew's activity including the extent of the drug operations here in Baltimore."

"So these people just handed over this information?"

"Actually yes. They are a really nice couple; they even turned over the seventy five thousand dollars along with the guns and drugs that they found."

"Wow. So how did you get the information and why are you here?"

"Well, the local police turned the info over to the District Attorney's office in N.Y. with whom I happen to have a very good relationship with. A friend of mines in the D.A.'s office knew I was following your case, so the file was given to me."

"Oh shit. That's what's up. So when do I get out of here?" I asked excitedly.

"Well it's not that simple. While the records *do* indicate the crew's heavy drug activity out here, unfortunately, they *don't* state that you were not an active member or *not* directly involved."

"What the fuck, but you said D-Boy left records," I responded raising my voice slightly.

"Yes he did and they incriminated the crew but again, the records did not say that you were not directly involved in any of the illegal activities."

"Well what did they say about me then?"

"They didn't say too much except that on quite a few occasions D-Boy dropped money and packages off to you."

"Yeah, well the money was Travon's and the packages were boxes of CD's, or at least that's what I was told."

"You mean you never checked?"

"No. I never had a reason to. He was my man and I trusted him."

"I believe you. Now we have to pray that we can find a judge that will."

"Okay. So what now?"

"Now you wait and pray while I try and cut through the red tape and get you out of here."

"I appreciate it, but I have to warn you, I have no money to pay you."

"That's okay. I'm working your case Pro-Bono."

"Thank you and I'm really grateful, but why are you doing this for me?"

"A few years ago, my father revealed to me that I had a sister living in another state, but she didn't grow up having all the luxuries and opportunities I was given. She was naïve just like you and got caught up in the fast life just like you. Unfortunately, she was killed before I had a chance to help her."

"Wow. I'm sorry to hear that."

"Yeah well, you just stay alive in here long enough to be saved."

"Oh, trust me. I'm all good in here."

"Okay good. Oh and two more things. Don't tell anybody about this and when or if you ever get out of here, lay low. If Travon finds out the case is re-opened, he is likely to get rid of all loose ends starting with you."

"Kill me. Nah, Travon would never do anything to hurt me."

"And you say this while serving a million years in jail behind him. Unbelievable. You haven't learned a damn thing. GUARD!"

With that being said, she slammed her business card on the table then got up and left. Damn she was right. What possessed those dumb ass words to come out of my mouth? I wanted to kick my own ass for even saying that shit accidentally. But one thing's for sure, if she was right and Travon would come looking to harm me, he would have another thing coming.

THE SECOND COMING

It had been almost four months since Sophia visited me with the news. Since then she has visited me a few times and wrote numerous letters keeping me updated on the status of my case. Despite all of the new evidence, shockingly every judge that she presented the case to had turned us down. She advised me to keep my head up and insisted that the fight was far from over. I promised her that I would try not to get discouraged and I planned to keep my promise; however over the past four months I did manage to break one promise, I had to tell Monica about the possibility of me coming home. She was my sister and I knew she would keep it tight. I didn't even tell Michelle who had been released two months ago. Monica seemed like she was more excited than I was, but I told her to chill until shit was official.

I was in my cell reading a book by author Sean A. Wright, when Washington came and tapped on the wall with her nightstick.

"Let's go book worm. You got a visitor."

It was Monday so it must have been Sophia.

"Girl shut the hell up, ain't nobody no book worm," I joked as we walked towards the visiting room. As we

33

approached the room, Sophia sat there with a somber look on her face that had my morning chow doing cartwheels in the pit of my stomach.

"Hey Sophie, what's up?" I asked as she stood and gave me a hug.

"Hey Tiff. Sit down sweetie," she said sounding as if the world was about to end.

"Okay, but I'm not liking the sound of this," I replied as I sat down hesitantly.

"Now listen Tiff, I don't want you to get all upset and riled up. I'm going to need you to keep your head up and maintain your composure," she said with a heavy heart.

I immediately lost it.

"What Sophia? Just spit it the fuck out. What? Did you drive four hours just to tell me that the system shitted on me again? Well fuck this fucked up ass system," I screamed, as I hurled a chair across the room.

Two C.O.'s rushed in but Sophia waved them off.

"Tiffany! Listen to me, pull yourself together and calm down before they throw your ass in the hole and the only way to avoid that is by going back to your cell and packing your things. You're going home Tiffany.

"Look, I don't give a fuck. Wait. What did you say?" I stuttered as her last statement smacked the shit out of me.

"I said you're going home Tiffany. We did it," she exclaimed grabbing my hands as my eyes immediately welled up with tears and then began to overflow.

"Oh my God, I can't believe it. What? How? Oh shit, my legs are getting weak."

"Well then sit down silly so I can explain."

34

I sat down and began to fan myself as I listened intensely to her every word.

"Okay. You caught a break. The New York District Attorney's office is working in conjunction with the Baltimore task force. The Baltimore authorities have reviewed the new information and have agreed to release you, contingent on the New York task force diligently pursuing a case against Travon."

"That's what's up. They need to lock his ass up and throw away the fuckin' key."

"Well, it's not going to be easy. New York is pulling strings to get you out, but they know they are going to have a hard time indicting Travon, because as you know he is good at what he does and they can never get enough evidence to make anything stick. They have been trying for a very long time."

"Okay. Well fuck him, when can I leave?" I asked ready to pack my shit right then and there.

"Well the process has been started, so a week, maybe two, give or take."

" This is really official right? I'm actually going home?" I asked just to make sure.

"Yes Tiffany, but I implore you; when you get out, get low and stay low, and for God's sake stay out of New York and away from Travon Outlaw. As far as Travon knows you are rotting in jail, so let's keep it that way. A dead man tells no tales."

"Don't worry, get me out of here and I'm a ghost. Believe that!"

"Let's hope so, trust me it's for your own good."

FREE AT LAST

Monica picked me up in a cherry red Aston Martin that she *borrowed* from some dummy she was dealing with.

"What's up you jailbird bitch?" she joked sitting on the hood of the car as I exited the gates.

"That's ex-jailbird bitch, now shut the hell up and help me with these boxes," I responded with a chuckle.

"Damn are those the new Gucci boxes? I gotta get me some of them," she continued to joke.

"Whatever, it ain't like I got a choice. They make you take this shit with you," I said as we loaded the small boxes into the trunk.

After loading the last of the boxes into the trunk, Monica gave me a much needed hug. It was long and heartfelt. I had not had one of those in over four years, not since the last time that nigga Travon held me, which subsequently was the same night the Feds kicked my motherfucking door in.

"Girl I am so glad this shit is over," I said as tears streamed down my face.

"Me too. Four years without my star pupil and number one rider has been a hurt piece."

"Well I'm back for good, so let's ride out," I said as we got in the car and pulled off.

We rode in silence for a few minutes as I took advantage of the scenery and free air that I was breathing. I was lost in my own thoughts when I felt the car slowing down and pulling over.

"What's up? Why we pulling over?" I asked a bit perplexed.

"Gotta stop at the ATM right quick, open the glove box."

I opened the glove box, but didn't see anything but the insurance and the registration.

"Okay, I don't see shit."

"Bitch look harder, there's a small blue envelope."

"Oh that. Okay I got it."

"Well open it."

I opened the envelope and saw an ATM card with my name on it. I sat there with a confused look on my face.

"Well don't just sit there. Go swipe that motherfucker and get you some bread."

I was still in shock as I exited the car and headed to the ATM machine that we were parked in front of. As I approached the ATM machine I inserted the card and was immediately prompted to enter my pin number. I turned around and Monica already knew what I wanted.

"0806 the month and year we met," she yelled from the car.

I smiled and turned back around and punched in the numbers. I then instinctively hit the view balance button. My mouth dropped open as it revealed a sum of nineteen thousand, four hundred seventy six dollars and seventy-eight cents. I counted the zeros and the commas again to make sure I wasn't tripping. When I was sure that I wasn't I turned around.

"Yo. What the fuck?" I asked still in shock.

"I'll explain later, just get some bread and let's go."

I turned back around and proceeded to take out five hundred dollars in three separate transactions, since fifteen hundred dollars was the max amount the ATM would give in one day. Once I collected the money and the receipt I returned to the car.

"Girl, what the hell is going on?"

"Nothing really, it's just that over the past four years each and every time I got my hands on some bread, I broke off a piece and put it up for you. When it was time to put money on ya books, I took half from your account and half from mines. I was gonna do that until my casket dropped bitch. I never expected you to hit these streets again."

"Wow. That's why I fucks with you. Now let's go so I can get out of these clothes.

"Uh yeah, that look is soooo two thousand seven, but I gotta go home first."

"Whatever bitch, just drive," I replied playfully punching her in the arm.

MOVIN' ON UP

When we arrived at Monica's new house I was once again in total shock. She told me she moved to a better neighborhood, but damn, I hadn't seen another black person in the last ten minutes but in the Homeland section of Maryland that was not surprising. Monica told me that in order to upgrade her lifestyle; she would have to upgrade her choice of men. So now her stable was full of nothing but of blue-collar men that consisted of Doctors, Engineers and niggas with 401k plans (Unfortunately no Attorneys, but that didn't matter now.)

The new crib was a three bedroom; split level Townhouse with a two-car garage. One spot was for her very own Mercedes S500 and the other spot was for whatever car she decided to "borrow" from one of her new breed of sponsors.

"Damn girl. This shit is hot. You definitely did the damn thing," I said complimenting her on the house.

"Thanks, but wait till you see how I laced the inside."

She led the way up to the large white double doors with gold handles and one way frosted glass. She opened the door; we stepped into the foyer and she deactivated the alarm as we instinctively took our shoes off.

"That's right bitch, you know the drill," she joked.

"Oh shut up and give me the grand tour."

She led me up a short flight of steps where both walls were lined with pictures of the Stiletto Divas in our hay day. I grinned from ear to ear as I reminisced on the first real friends that I ever had. I was overjoyed and couldn't wait to be reunited with my sisters, and then it hit me; damn. Lashawn moved away, then it hit me harder, Terri was dead. I was suddenly overcome with grief as I stopped and thought of my fallen sister. Monica got to the top of the steps and realized I wasn't behind her. She noticed the look on my face.

"C'mon Tiff. You have to move on and celebrate your life. I don't mean to sound all cle'shaish and shit but Terri would have wanted it that way."

I sniffled a little bit as tears raced down my face. Next to Monica Terri was my bitch and she was gone. I wiped my tears and continued to the top of steps only to be slapped in the face again by a giant oil painting of us that hung over her fireplace. The tears tried to start up again, but I forced them back in, as I looked around at the all white ensemble that looked like I had just stepped into the Antarctic.

"Damn. It's blinding in here. I don't know whether to sit down, or build a snow man," I joked.

"That's right. All white errthang. Just like the song goes."

"Mmm mmm mmm. Well what did you come to get? I need to go shopping, get my nails done and do something with my hair."

"Well let me show you something first."

She led me through the house, passed the dining room with the table large enough to seat fifteen people, passed the all black kitchen, passed the large room with the pool table with balls made out of crystal. She then led me up the winding staircase to a large bedroom that contained a king sized bed, with a fifty-six inch LCD television that hung from the wall. There was a large bathroom with two sinks and two very large vanities. It had a standalone shower with multiple showerheads, and a Jacuzzi that seemed like it was big enough for about four people. The bathroom was decorated in lavender and white. This spot was definitely fit for a queen.

"Damn this shit is hot," I admitted complimenting her on her beautiful room.

"C'mon now. You know how I do. Check the closets."

I opened up the closet and I was amazed to see the contents of the walk in closet. It was full on both sides with designer clothes, shoes, and bags. The closet seemed to go on forever.

"Wow. This looks like my old closet. Ain't no drugs and guns under the floorboard is it? " I joked half heartedly.

"Bitch. If I had all that shit, trust, it would be in my own closet."

"Uhhh this is your closet dumb ass," I chuckled.

"Uhhh no silly bitch. This actually *your* room and all the clothes and shit are brand new, the tags are still on them and they're yours too. I got the pants a size bigger. All them chow hall starches got you a lil' thicker over the years."

"Oh shut the hell up. I only went up one size and I still look good. No stomach, no nothing, so thanks for the wardrobe, but I can't believe you gave me your master bedroom. That was a nice addition to all of the welcome home gifts."

"Bitch please. This is the guest room and you can fit two of these in my bedroom. Now shower, change and do something with you ya wig so we can roll out."

"Oh word, it's like that? Where we going?"

"Don't worry. Just get dressed."

BUSINESS AS USUAL

"Listen motherfucker. I pay you more than enough money to make shit like this go away. Now the next call I get better be you telling me this shit has been taken care of."

I slammed the phone down in frustration and laid back against the headboard.

"What was that about Travon?" my wife Janelle asked, sounding just as frustrated as I was.

"Same shit, different day. This D.A wants me bad. Every time I turn around he is grasping at straws to find a reason to lock me up."

"Well don't expect no sympathy from me. I've been telling you for years to leave them streets alone and you just refuse to listen. How long do you think the law is gonna let you keep spitting in they face? You ain't gonna be happy till they lock ya dumb ass up."

I had heard enough of her lecturing.

"You know, you sure do talk a lot of shit for somebody who helps spend all this money. I don't hear yo ass complaining about how I get it while you pushing your Benz or my Bentley and I damn sure don't see you looking for work when the bill from Gucci comes in at like ten stacks a month. So miss me with the bullshit Janelle."

45

"Motherfucker, I am your wife and we have kids that need to be provided for. I don't complain about the way the money comes in because it ain't like you gonna quit and get a legit job and far be it from me to think you would invest your money in anything besides fucking drugs," she snapped, now raising her voice.

"Lower your motherfuckin' voice Tiffany, before the kids hear you," I said through clenched teeth, not realizing what I had just said.

"Who the fuck did you just call me, you sorry motherfucker? Are you serious? Four years later and you still got Tiffany on the fucking brain? Un-fucking believable. I should have divorced yo ass when all that shit went down in Baltimore. And you know what? It ain't just the fact that you fucked another broad; you had a whole relationship with her and got her pregnant. Here is something else that I have been holding back since all of that happened. I have never looked at you the same after you left that poor girl stuck holding the bag. That sweetie was a straight pussy move."

It was only because she was the mother of my children that she didn't pick herself up off of the floor after that last statement but I wasn't gonna lay there and take it. I got up, grabbed the keys to my Range Rover and left as she continued to spew insults. I knew I fucked up by calling her Tiffany. But the truth of the matter is, what I did to Tiffany never sat well with me either. Contrary to what her friends and the rest of the people who watch the news may think, I did love Tiffany. I will even go as far as to say I had truly fallen in love with her. I regret not keeping it real with her about who I was and what I really did for a living. I robbed her of her right to choose and a part of me hated myself for that, and maybe that's why I couldn't get her out of my mind, even after four years. But I had to shake it off because at the end of the day I was a hustler and self-preservation is the first rule of survival. I had completely forgotten that rule until I was faced down on the floor that day with the handcuffs on me. The day my best friend in the world set me up, was the same day I was forced to set up the love of my life and the mother of my unborn child. And that is the reason I blew his motherfuckin' face off outside of the courthouse. I did that for Tiffany.

After driving around for what seemed like forever, I pulled up in front of my club Visions. I had purchased it when I decided to stay close to home after D-Boy totally fucked up the Baltimore operation. I missed him too, but he had to go. I have zero tolerance for treason and a below zero tolerance for snitches. So on that note, fuck 'em. Lorenzo was the only one who stayed true to the game, so I kept him on board. The majority of the crew was handpicked by D-Boy, so I let them all go. And as far as L.V. goes, Lorenzo made sure no one would ever see him again. Well they would, but it would probably be piece by piece. I never liked that motherfucker anyway; he was D's man, not mines.

I pulled into my reserved parking spot right in front of the club. Business was booming as usual and the line was around the corner. As I approached the club the bouncer unhooked the red velvet rope and ushered me inside. Once inside, I acknowledged a few staff members and patrons as I made my way through the crowd towards the private

47

staircase in the rear of the club that lead up to my office. The hulking security guard that blocked the staircases name was Sayeed. He stood about six feet five inches tall and weighed about two hundred and seventy five pounds and I'm guessing almost no body fat. I had him posted there because these streets was crazy and although I had no problem holding my own, if a motherfucker tried to get at me here at the club they would have to go through Sayeed first, and not many people would be up to the challenge.

"What's up boss man?" he asked as I approached.

"Ain't shit, just getting to this money."

"I can dig it."

"Nobody comes up unannounced except Lorenzo and Shanise."

"No doubt."

I continued up the steps, unlocked my office and proceeded inside. I took my Desert Eagle out of my waistband and placed it on my mahogany desk. I then proceeded over to my private bar and poured a triple shot of white Henny. I grabbed the universal remote off of the coffee table and sat back on my black plush Italian leather couch. I turned on the basketball game and my closed circuit security system that showed me almost every square inch of the club. I was just about to take a sip of my drink when my cell phone rang. It was Lorenzo.

"What's good my dude?" I asked as I picked up.

"*Ain't shit. I handled that B.I. for you.*"

"A'ight cool. I'm at the club swing through."

"*A'ight bet. Give me a few.*"

"No doubt. Good looking."

After completing the call, I took the drink to the head and turned my attention to the Knicks vs. Heat game. I looked up just in time to see Carmello Anthony break Lebron James' ankles and score to put the Knicks up by three with forty-two seconds left in the game. Miami called a timeout and that was perfect because I needed another drink. I went over to the bar, poured the drink and went and sat back on the couch and just as the game came back on there was a knock at my office door.

"Fuck!" I said out loud.

I looked at the video monitor and saw that it was Shanise. I wanted to make her wait and finish watching the game but business comes first. I paused the game on my DVR and went to let her in. She walked in wearing a black form fitting Herve Leger dress that accentuated her bangin' ass shape and had her thirty four double DD's pouring out of the top. Her hips were stretching the sides and her ass was trying to make a run for it out the back. But as hot as she looked standing there in her five-inch heels, and her hair that stopped right below her neck, nothing looked better than the large Hermes pocketbook she was carrying and the contents inside.

"Hey Tray," she said as she kissed me on the check and walked passed me.

I followed her over to the table as she emptied the contents of the pocketbook.

"Here you go baby, two bricks of yay and fifty-six stacks," she counted out.

"Hold up, the count is supposed to be sixty-thousand even."

"Yeah well, they was short again. That's why I brought two of the bricks back."

"Yo, that's the fourth time this month they been fuckin' short. What the fuck is going on out there in Baisley?"

"Baby they been slippin' ever since Black Rob got booked. You gonna have to send a message to tighten they ass's up."

I immediately got defensive.

"Are you telling me how to run my fuckin' business Shanise?"

"No daddy, of course not. All I'm saying is they obviously think shit is sweet. Now you know I have no problem at all putting the heat to any of them niggas, but that's not in my job description. You always ask my opinion, so I'm giving it to you. Lorenzo and Sayeed need to take a trip out to Baisley Projects and holla at that nigga Bruno."

She was right. And that's why I fucked with her. *Shanise was the most thorough bitch I knew. She was originally from Gary, Indiana, but she knew that it was much too slow out there for the type of life she wanted, so she caught some nigga slippin' out there for like ten stacks and a few pounds of weed. She jumped in her Chrysler Aspen hit the highway headed for New York and never looked back. She didn't know anybody here so obviously she had no connections. I happened to meet her about two years ago on her third day here, at Lucille's Diner on the late night. She was sitting at the back booth all by herself. Her beauty caught me as soon as I walked in the door. I nodded to the manager signaling that I wanted the usual and headed straight back to her. I introduced myself and we hit it off. I wanted a dime to take my mind off Janelle and her bullshit, and she wanted a boss nigga that she could start a new life with. I bought the weed from her and took her under my wing. For a few months we just fucked and enjoyed each other's company until she showed me that she was an asset and not just some ass. Once she showed me her hustle skills and that she knew how to handle her own on any level I made our relationship strictly business.*

"You're a hundred percent right and that's why I keep you around," I said as I tossed her three grand and sat back down on the couch.

Without counting the money, she put it in her purse and turned to me.

"No nigga. You keep me around because your wife don't know what to do with a thorough ass nigga like you and you know I'm willing to do everything she does and more," she confessed as she straddled my lap.

I picked her up off of my lap and placed her beside me. I was doing really good with the whole not mixing business and pleasure thing. After I had to cancel that bitch Tracy's contract I started learning to separate the two. So as bad as I wanted Shanise in every way, I would hate to have to kill her.

"C'mon Ma, you know we been stopped the business and pleasure thing."

"Okay then I quit," she said playfully stroking my chin.

"You can't. You one of my top earners. Now get ya pretty ass out there and earn."

"Uh whatever. I am done for the evening. I believe fifty six stacks is great for one nights worth of work."

Before I could respond, there was a knock at the door. The video monitor showed it was Lorenzo.

"Go let him in," I instructed.

She did what she was told and Lorenzo came in with a sense of urgency.

"I'm glad both of ya'll are here. I just heard some crazy shit."

PANDORA'S BOX

After I got showered and did something to my hair, I threw on a hot ass Dolce' outfit with matching stiletto's of course, then Monica took me out to a nice expensive restaurant. We were laughing and reminiscing but about half way through the bottle of Moscato Monica got all serious on me.

"Tiff you know you my girl right?"

"Of course I do. And you know you my bitch too, now pass the bottle."

"No. Let's chill on the bottle for a minute. We need to talk," she replied in the most serious tone I had ever heard her in.

"What the hell is wrong with you?" I asked, very concerned.

"Remember when you first got caught up in that bullshit and you made me promise to never bring it up again?"

"Yeah I remember. Even though I was in jail, I wanted to forget everything that happened."

"Well for the first time ever I need to break a promise to you."

"No, No, No. Fuck that. You promised and I can't take re-hashing that shit. DO NOT do this to me Monica," I pleaded.

"Look. You ain't the only one that was affected by this shit. You think you were the only one that did that four year bid. You don't think I was locked up with you," she revealed.

"Locked up with me? Locked up with me? Are you fucking serious. So I guess the only man you ever loved shitted on you, set you up and sent you to jail for a million fucking years. Oh yeah and I forgot you lost your unborn baby from the stress of your fucking world crashing down on you. Yeah you right Monica. You were right there in my cell with me."

"Wow. You gonna fix your lips to say some shit like that to me Tiff?"

I slammed my fork down on my plate.

"Okay. Fuck it. Spit it out. What is so important Monica? What is so important that you can't leave the past in the god damn past?"

"Look, ain't nobody trying to pour salt in your open wounds. I'm just saying some things just can't be locked away forever. I mean I have questions just like everyone else Tiffany."

"What questions? Haven't I answered enough questions? Damn!"

"To the law and the media maybe, but what about me? Are you just gonna leave me in the dark?"

"Leave you in the dark about what? What is there to tell Monica?"

"Well for starters, what's been going through your mind these past four years? I mean, I haven't seen you shed one tear or show any emotion since the day of the trial."

"It's hard to show emotion when you've become emotionless. That whole situation left me numb, and made me cold and bitter. So that makes my thoughts cold and bitter, and I'm sure you don't wanna hear about those."

"As a matter of fact I do. Let's hear those cold, bitter, thoughts Tiff."

"Let it go Monica."

"No Tiffany, you can't keep that shit bottled up. You gotta let it out before you explode."

"You pushing it Monica. Check please," I yelled to the waiter as my eyes began to well up with tears.

"We don't need the fucking check. We still talking," she snapped waiving the waiter off.

"What Monica? What the fuck do you wanna know?" I asked, now frustrated and desperately fighting back an onslaught of tears.

"You're home, you're free, but you did all that time for something you didn't do. You lost your freedom and your baby. Stop holding back and let it out."

That's all I could take. I exploded.

"Okay, you wanna know my motherfucking thoughts? I wanna kill that motherfucker and I hate you for introducing me to this lifestyle," I screamed making a scene while throwing the rest of my drink in her face and running out of the restaurant in tears. I made it to the curb and hailed a cab before she was able to catch up to me. I took the taxi home, put on my nightgown and cried myself to sleep.

A soft tap on my shoulder awakened me. I rolled over to see Monica standing there with eyeliner tracks streaming down her face where tears used to be.

"Hey Chica," she said with a solemn smile on her face.

"Oh my god Monica, I am so sorry. I was way out of pocket, and I didn't mean any of the things I said to you earlier. You have been nothing but good to me from day one, and the only person besides my parents to ever hold me down."

"You know Tiffany, after you threw that drink in my face, my first instinct was to snatch you up and rip it up with you but I decided to chill and take a long drive instead. I replayed your words over and over again in my mind, and the truth of the matter is you were right. When I met you, I knew you wasn't built for this shit. I mean, some broads are a little rough around the edges and I smooth them out to fit this lifestyle, but you had no business running with us. I preyed on your looks and your innocence and totally fucked your life up. I'm the one that should be sorry, not you. So I wanna say I'm sorry and I love you girl," she said in between sniffles.

"I thought the number one rule was to love nobody but yourself?" I asked as we faced each other with tears in our eyes.

"Listen Tiffany, fuck all the…"

I cut her off by grabbing her face and passionately kissing her. I laid her back on the bed and unbuttoned her blouse, then took each thirty-eight D's in my mouth and made love to them with my tongue. I watched as her nipples

56

tripled in size before my eyes. Her panting and heavy breathing confirmed her appreciation. It had been four long years since I was this passionate about anything, and I intended on conveying that to her with my actions. I unbuckled her pants and attempted to slide them down but she stopped me

"Yo Tiff chill."

Her rejection immediately fucked me up.

"Huh. Why, what's wrong?" I asked perplexed.

She immediately turned away from me.

"Just chill Tiff, this shit ain't cool?" she whispered still not looking at me.

"I don't get it. You have been trying to fuck me since you first met me. So now's your chance. What's the problem?"

"Tiff your like my sister. Let's just not cross the line okay?"

I sensed something wasn't right, but I wasn't gonna push the issue so I let it go.

"Okay my bad. Well since you're already in here, can you at least just lay here with me? Besties do that all the time."

"Yeah I can do that. Move your big ass over."

She laid down behind me and draped her arm over me.

"Tiffany, can I ask you one more question?"

"Sure go head."

"Have you heard anything about Travon since all that shit went down?"

"Nope, not a fucking word. Have you?"

"Nah. It's like that nigga just disappeared off the face of the earth."

"Good. I hope that motherfucker fell face first into hell."

"You're crazy girl. So what would you do if you did know where he was?"

"Girl I wouldn't do shit. I would stay as far away from that nigga as possible."

"Yeah I feel you. That's a good idea."

"Hey. What's up with the Travon questions all of a sudden?

"Huh. Nothing girl, just making conversation. Good night."

"Good night."

The next morning I woke up in the bed alone, to the smell of breakfast being cooked. I put on my robe and headed down to the kitchen. As I got closer I could hear Monica on her cell phone.

"No trust me. I had a long talk with her last night and she has no intention on coming up there, you're safe just keep doing what you're doing. Okay look, I gotta go so stop flirting and get back to business."

I stopped in my tracks when I heard the conversation. Maybe I was still half asleep and I didn't hear what I just thought I heard. I proceeded into the kitchen and Monica abruptly ended the call.

"Okay look, I gotta go. Bye! Good morning Tiff. Now look bitch, don't complain about the cooking. You know I ain't used to this shit."

I gave her a half assed fake laugh and went right in on her.

"So who was you talking to on the phone all early?" I asked mentally giving her the side eye.

"Oh girl that was just business as usual. Now get out of mines and eat your food."

Maybe she was right; I should just mind my business. How dare I even think that Monica would do me dirty? My thought process was totally out of pocket. I would dismiss the thought and try to stomach Monica's cooking.

OLD DOG, NEW TRICKS

I don't why I let Monica talk me into going on a double date with these two doctors. I wanted to stay home for two reasons. First off, I had too much on my mind and I was not in the mood to be socializing. Secondly and probably most important, I didn't do white boys. It's not that I was prejudice; it's just that they didn't turn me on. I hated how they acted when they are around a beautiful, black, stacked woman. They be all googley eyed, touchy feely, foaming at the mouth and shit. Ugghh! That shit made my skin crawl, but after everything that Monica had done for me hanging out for a few hours is the least I could do. I had on a black form fitting dress that showed my cleavage and the perfect roundness of my breasts. I wore red and black five-inch stiletto heels, and I carried a black and red Gucci clutch. Monica had on a black pantsuit with a white bustier top and white six-inch stilettos. Monica opted to drive and meet our dates at the restaurant as opposed to them coming to the house. That was considered a definite no no.

We pulled up in front of Fogo De Chao, a fancy Brazilian restaurant near the Baltimore Harbor. Monica gave the valet the keys and we headed inside where Roger and

Thomas were waiting for us. Roger was a Pediatrician and Thomas was a Gynecologist. I would get stuck with the damn pussy doctor.

Throughout the course of the night we ate, drank and listened to Roger and Thomas tell corny ass med school jokes and stories. I was getting agitated, as my predictions were proving true. I had to remove Thomas' hand from my thigh on more than one occasion. The food and drinks were excellent, but I couldn't wait to get the hell out of there and after about an hour more of drinks, bad jokes and groping that's exactly what we did. As we were waiting for the valet to bring our cars around Roger decided to further piss me off.

"Look ladies the night is still young. Why don't we go back to my condo and keep the party going? "

"Dude that is a sweet idea," Thomas joined in, co-signing.

"Thanks but no thanks. I'm getting sleepy so I better head home and get some sleep."

"Monica what's up with your homie? I thought you said she was cool?" Roger asked sounding a little agitated.

"She is cool, right Tiffany?" she said giving me that look.

"I guess I can hang out just a little while longer," I replied reluctantly.

"Sweet. You girls follow us. I hope your Benzo can keep up with my Maserati," Roger said winking at us.

When Monica and I got into her car she read my mind like she was Ms. Cleo.

"Just an hour Tiff I promise," she pleaded.

"One hour Monica, not a second more."

"Thanks girl you are the best."

"Mmm hmm."

We drove for about twenty-five minutes until we got to a gated community. We waited for Roger to input the pin code so that the gates could open. When they did, we had to hurry in right behind them so we would not get caught by the closing gates. We parked our cars and made our way up to the condo.

"Make yourselves at home," Roger said as he turned the lights on.

The condo was nice and expensively decorated. I was a little taken aback because there were family portraits and pictures of him and a woman I assumed to be his wife everywhere. Roger must have notices the look on my face.

"No worries. The wife and kids are in Paris for the next two weeks," he explained as if this was something he did on the regular.

"You sure we're going to be straight up in here?" I said not really feeling the situation.

"You girls are will be fine. I just have to make sure I clean up all of the loose weave strands when you leave," he said, being dead serious.

"What motherfucker? Neither one of us wear weave. It's all natural over here dickhead," I snapped back.

Monica was pissed because I snapped out before she did.

"Monica your friend is a little touchy. Why don't you and I head into the bedroom and leave her and Tommy alone to get more acquainted."

"She's cool, that was just some racist disrespectful shit. You luck one of us ain't crack the shit out of you."

"Be cool baby. There's no need for violence. I'll make it up to you when we get in the bed room," Roger said pulling on Monica's arm.

"I hope that's where you keep the safe, because that last remark is going to cost you," Monica replied.

"I know, and I am prepared to pay handsomely for my mistake."

"You good Tiffany?" Monica asked.

I didn't say a word. I just tapped my watch.

"I know, I know," Monica said, as she was lead away into the bedroom.

As soon as we were alone thirsty ass Thomas went right in on me.

"You mind if I sit next to you?" he asked sitting down before I could decline.

"Sure have a seat," I responded sarcastically.

"So I'm sure you noticed that I couldn't keep my eyes off you all night."

"Yeah, and your hands either," I snarled.

"I don't know what it is baby. You just do something to me."

"Okay, I think you've had a little too much to drink," I said attempting to get up and sit on the other couch before he grabbed my arm.

"White boy if you don't get the fuck off of me, I'm going to split your shit wide open," I seethed meaning every word of it.

"Look, I'm sorry. I'm just not sure how this works. Do I pay your first? Do we fuck first? I'm new at this."

"Motherfucker we ain't no damn prostitutes. That's it. I'm getting my girl and we are out of here."

"Wait. I'm not trying to offend you. I tell you what. We don't have to have sex. I'll give you fifteen hundred dollars just to let me snort some blow off of those nice juicy tits of yours."

This motherfucker was ill, but as long as there was no sex involved, I would play his game.

"Make it twenty five hundred, no touching and you got a deal."

"Will that be check or credit?"

"Cash motherfucker, straight cash," I said as I could hear Monica pretending to get her back blown out in the bedroom.

She owed me big time for this one.

THIEVES IN THE TEMPLE

"What's the problem fam?" I asked Lorenzo, noticing the urgency on his face and in his voice.

"Yo. I'm hearing that Bruno and them Baisley niggas been talkin' real reckless."

"Yeah they was short on today's pick-up too and they act like they ain't give a fuck either," Shanise chimed in.

"Okay we need to nip this shit in the bud now before it gets out of hand," I spat now getting agitated at the thought that Bruno was trying to play me."

"Well I just wanted to drop this bread off to you first, but I'mma take a few cats out there and tighten shit up," Lorenzo stated sounding more anxious than I was.

"No. I tell you what. We don't need that yet. Let's take a ride out there so I can holler at the youngster.

"You sure you don't want me to bring a few heads with us?"

"No. Me, you and Sayeed should be good enough. I don't anticipate the little nigga causing a problem."

"Well I'm coming too, so let's ride out Shanise said, pulling her pink .380 with the pearl handle out of her bag and cocking it back.

I grabbed my Desert Eagle and led the way out of my office. Once we got down the stairs I tapped Sayeed on the shoulder.

"Let's go big fella. We got some business to handle."

"Good. I was getting bored," Sayeed replied.

When we pulled up across the street from Baisley Projects, Bruno was leaned up against his white Porsche truck surrounded by his crew and a few broads. Instinctively we all checked our weapons and exited the vehicle. As we walked across the street, one of Bruno's boys tapped him on the shoulder and pointed in our direction. Bruno turned around just as we reached the curb.

"Oh shit. My nigga Travon. What you doin' slumming in the projects?" he said sarcastically as he half-heartedly dapped me up.

"I came to holler at you about our current business arrangement. Let's take a walk real quick son."

"Nah Bee, the walk ain't necessary. Anything you need to say you can say right here, this my family. Well the niggas is. You bitches beat it for a minute and let grown men talk," he said dismissing his female company.

"Okay look," I started before he cut me off.

"Hold up. I got rid of my bitches, now get rid of yours," he said referring to Shanise.

"I don't mind being a bitch but how you feel about being a pussy?" she spat back.

"Yo Travon. Put that broad in check. Anyway what's the deal?"

"You tell me Bruno. I mean the bread keep coming back with slices missing. What part of the game is that?"

"Aww nigga, all that cake you sitting on and you crying over a few stacks? It ain't like you need it. Cut that shit out fam'," he said nonchalantly.

"Oh you countin' my pockets now nigga? You know that ain't a wise thing to do. So the price of the package just went up, and it's gonna stay that way until you learn how to follow the rules of the game," I stated firmly.

"Nigga, you think you the only candy store in town?" he replied, angrily.

"Don't be silly, of course I am. Shanise will be by tomorrow to pick up the shorts from tonight and make sure we don't have this problem again, because you're right I don't like slumming."

With that being said we turned to leave. As we crossed the street I turned back around.

"And oh yeah. You need some air in ya back tire son."

Bruno inspected his truck tire.

"Ain't nothing wrong with my tire Bee."

I swiftly pulled out my Desert Eagle and sent a shot through his back tire.

"Now it is. Get that fixed fam."

He and his boys instinctively went for their weapons but Shanise, Lorenzo, and Sayeed, already had the drop on them.

"You wanna do it this way Bruno, or you wanna play nice?" I asked with a look that burned a hole right through his ego.

"Nah, it's all love Bee. I was getting new rims anyway. Everything is everything. Send shorty by tomorrow and we'll square up that tab," he replied with a disturbed look on his face.

As we started heading back across the street Lorenzo broke his silence.

"You know that nigga gonna be a problem right?"

"Well if so, I guess you got some overtime to put in."

"Oh no doubt, I'll rock a bye that nigga with no problem."

"Yeah well, let's hope it doesn't come to that."

CONNECTIONS

It had been a few weeks since my release and I was still getting re-adjusted to society. I also needed to figure out how I was going to start my life over. I mean, what Monica did for me financially was cool, but that money wouldn't last long. I needed to formulate a plan quickly. I thought about opening up another salon, but I refused to step foot back in Baltimore, and the high profile people in this neighborhood didn't want a young black woman fooling around in they hair.

I was going through some of my letters and pictures that Monica had sent me while I was locked up. I laughed silently at some of the pictures and the content of the letters. Monica was definitely a piece of work. I was shuffling through the pictures when a piece of paper slipped out and fell to the floor. I picked it up and noticed that it was Michelle's phone number and address; I forgot that she had mailed it to me when she got out. I was about to throw it away then decided; fuck it let me give her a call. I grabbed my cell and dialed the number on the paper. After a couple rings, a female picked up.

"*Hello?*"

"Hello can I speak to Michelle please?"

"This is Michelle, but if you calling about that bum ass nigga Bobby, ain't nobody fucked ya man, nobody want ya man, and nobody thinking about ya man, and another thing bitch..."

I cut off her tirade.

"Whoa, whoa, chill it's me Tiffany?"

"Tiffany who?" she asked still agitated.

"Tiffany from Cumberland bitch. Who else?"

"Hold on, I didn't hear the operator say this was a call from the Feds."

"That's because I'm not in the Feds, I'm home."

"Oh my god. For real? Hold up girl. Who you snitch on?"

"Hoe don't play ya'self. Let's just say I got out on a technicality," I responded offended by the remark.

"Damn, that's what's up. I can't believe you're out. I was actually thinking about you the other day."

"Yeah. What was ya silly ass thinking about?"

"Well girl I got some deep shit to tell you, but not over the phone where are you?"

"I'm around. Why what's up?" I responded not wanting to give away my location.

"Meet me at Phillip's down by the harbor in an hour."

"Damn. What's with all the secret squirrel shit?" I asked getting agitated.

"Let's just say I've got some info about our past that I think you may want."

Now I was curious.

"Okay. I'll see you in an hour," I said as I hung up.

I went to ask Monica to borrow her car, but she was knocked out so I just took the keys off of her nightstand knowing that she wouldn't mind. Once inside the car I immediately turned on the GPS because I still didn't know my way around the new neighborhood. Once the GPS was on, I decide that rather than typing in my destination, I would just browse the search history because I knew Monica loved the harbor. As I filtered through the searches, I noticed a few New York destinations, this girl really got around. I found the coordinates of the harbor and hit the road.

When I arrived at Phillips', Michelle was sitting on the patio sipping a glass of Long Island Iced Tea. She saw me approaching, started smiling and got up to greet me.

"Heeeeey baby. Look at you. What's up?" she asked hugging me and kissing me on the cheek.

"You looking good. What's going on?" I asked wanting to get right down to the purpose of the meeting.

"Girl, sit down. This is some heavy shit."

I sat down and listened eagerly.

"Okay, spit it out," I said anxiously.

"Okay well listen. You know when I got out the pen, finding a gig was bitch. I mean girl I looked all over. I even lowered my standards and tried the fast food thing, but girl with that grease and shit in my nails and that hair net fuckin' up my doo I quit in like three days. Then I tried the whole stripping thing, but niggas want too much for too little. And after that I..."

I had to cut her off.

"Bitch will you get to the point? Ain't nobody drive no hour to hear ya' fuckin' resume," I snapped.

"Okay, I know where your ex is at," she spat quickly as if she was thought I was about to get up and leave.

Her statement smacked the shit out of me.

"What did you just say?"

"Ya' boy Travon Outlaw. Ain't that the nigga that did you dirty on them charges?"

"What do you know about Travon? And how do you have any info on him?"

"Well after I couldn't find a gig, I went back to what I do best, you know fucking with the I.D's and shit. So you know after I started getting my bread up, I started traveling in big circles. So one weekend I end up in New York at this party and I meet this nigga named Bruno who, as it turns out get's all of his coke from Travon and how do I know this? Well, he's cocky he just runs his mouth and he despises Travon so much that he just tells all of his business. So after the first time I heard him speak about him, I started plucking him for info which wasn't too hard once I threw this good shit on him."

"Holy shit. So what do you know?" I asked shocked at the info.

"I know he has a club, I know he has a wife and kids and I know he is running shit in New York. I seen him face to face. Tiffany that nigga look good and he got that gwap. I see how you got caught up."

"What bitch?"

"Oh shit. My bad Tiff, but I been around him a few times. Bruno likes to show me of when he fly's me up top. And he always takes me to Travon's club and makes himself known by buying out the bar in the V.I.P. section. He be trying to show Travon that his money is long too, but he's too dumb to realize that the money he's spending in the club is going right to Travon's ass."

"What does this dude Bruno know about you? And have you *ever* mentioned my name?"

"Girl he don't know shit about me or what I do and I never mentioned your name at all."

"I need you to really think hard. Have you ever mentioned me at all?"

"Tiff I swear, I wouldn't do that to you. And what would be the purpose of it? I just found out today that you were home."

"Exactly. All the more reason for you to be like, "oh I know Travon's girl, I was locked up with her, he did her dirty"...etc.

"Not at all baby. I was actually gonna mail you all of this info when I got around to it. I would imagine you want some get back."

"Yeah, you got that shit right. Look girl I appreciate the info. I'm gonna call you."

"No doubt. After all you did for me while we was at Cumberland, I feel I owe you my life. I came home to nothing or nobody so I hold on to how you took care of me."

"Well I'm home now, so you gonna be okay trust me. Look I gotta run. I will hit you up later," I said as I leaned over the table, gave her a kiss and turned to leave.

I got in the car and took a deep breath as I was overwhelmed by a ball of emotions. I fought back tears but couldn't tell if they were from anger or sadness. My hands were trembling as I fumbled to put the key in the ignition. Once the car was started I pulled off into the Baltimore traffic. About 20 minutes into my ride, Monica called my cell.

"Hello?"

"Bitch did you steal my car?" she joked.

"No girl. Not at all," I said solemnly.

"What's wrong?" she asked, detecting the tone of my voice.

"I'll explain when I get home. Shit just got real."

It seemed like it took me forever to make it back to the house. It was probably because my mind was racing with this newly acquired info on Travon. I was confused about a lot of things, but one thing I was sure of was the fact that when I dropped this info on Monica, she would help me formulate a plan for some get back on this motherfucker.

I pulled up, parked and entered the house where I immediately smelled weed and when I got to the top of the steps the aroma was confirmed. Monica was laid across the couch blowing some exotic.

"Girl, where the hell you been?" she asked taking a long pull.

"You wouldn't believe me if I told you."

"Spit it out, I'm all ears," she said still lying down.

"Girl I know where to find that nigga Travon."

Monica jumped up as if I said I knew where to find Tupac and Biggie.

"What? Where?" she said sounding just as, if not more excited than I was.

"Yeah girl, remember my celly Michelle that I used to always tell you about?"

"Yeah. What about her?"

"Well to make a long story short. When she got out, apparently she hooked up with some dudes from up top that are heavily affiliated with Travon's bitch ass."

"Who? What are the names?" she asked anxiously.

"I can't remember right now, but apparently the dude she fucks with gets all of his work from Travon. He knows his hangouts, his clubs, cars etc."

"Okay so why are you so excited?"

"Now I can reach out and fuck his life up, just like he did mines."

"What? No Tiff. Leave that man be," she said excitedly and defensively.

"What do you mean leave him alone? I finally got a chance for some get back on his punk ass, and you want me to let it ride?"

"Well that's what you said you were gonna do."

"Yeah, well that was when I thought I'd never see his bitch ass again and now that I got the element of surprise on him, I'm gonna tear his shit out the frame."

"Listen, I know you hype and everything, but you playing a dangerous game right now. I think you need to take a deep breath and re-evaluate your motherfucking thought process. I mean seriously, what you gonna do, knock on his door and blow his fuckin' head off?"

"If need be and why the fuck are you trying to talk me down? I asked raising my voice and now getting agitated.

"I'm simply saying that you're a free woman now and you should leave well enough alone. Take this shit as a lesson and move on with your life."

"Look, I did learn a lesson and that was to never let anyone take advantage of me again. That motherfucker left me to rot and die in prison for some shit I didn't even know was going down. Now that I got a chance for some payback, you want me to leave it alone? Fuck outta here. Now either you with me, or you against me," I said with a look and tone I had never used before.

"Of course I'm with you but...."

"Ain't no butts, I'm gonna figure this shit out and we gonna make a move on that nigga."

"Okay Tiff, but I'm simply saying this shit could cost you your life," she pleaded.

"I doubt it. He can't kill me twice," I said as I walked away.

NIP IT IN THE BUD

It had been a few weeks since my little run in with that nigga Bruno and while the money was coming back straight, he was still talkin' slick about me in the streets and that is something that could not and would not be tolerated. So I called a meeting at the club with Sayeed, Lorenzo, and Shanise. When I got there, they were already in my office waiting. When I walked in, they stood up.

"Chill, ya'll sit down, " I said as I headed straight to the bar to pour myself a shot. I took it to the head and then started the meeting.

"So what do today's numbers look like?" I asked surveying the room.

"40 projects and Sutphin Blvd. are all good," Lorenzo reported.

"Rockaway Blvd and Baisley are all in pocket," Shanise chimed in.

"Cool. Any short money?" I asked.

"Nah." They both said simultaneously.

"Everything is accounted for and waiting for you over there in that bag," Lorenzo added.

"Okay cool. Now on to our next order of business. Word on the street is this nigga Bruno is still talkin' reckless," I said with a sense of urgency.

"Aww let the lil' nigga talk. That shit ain't stopping our bread so fuck 'em," Lorenzo responded.

"Yeah, niggas are always gonna hate on you, but as long as the cash keeps flowing they can eat a dick," Shanise added.

"Yeah I feel ya'll on that but when the money is gone all you have left is your name and my mother always says that your name will take you further than a dollar any day. So with that being said, we gotta nip this shit in the bud. That nigga Bruno needs a slight spanking," I ordered.

"Okay. I feel you on that and you the boss Tray, but as your second in command I have to advise you that as much of a pain in the ass that nigga Bruno may be, a good percentage of our income comes from him and his crew in Baisley. Them niggas get it in out there. So starting a war would be like cutting our nose off to spite our face," Lorenzo advised.

"Yeah that makes sense, but at the same time Bruno ain't no dummy. He knows he ain't getting product like mines from nowhere else. I'm the only candy store in town and as far as going to war; I ain't worried because Bruno ain't even built like that. My grandmother used to say, a monkey knows what branch to jump on," I responded as I paced the floor.

"Yo you killing me with all these Outlaw family quotes and shit," Shanise joked, as we all chuckled.

"Okay. So what's the plan?" Sayeed asked breaking his silence.

"It's simple. We take another ride out to Baisley, but we make our message a little more firm this time," I responded pouring another shot.

"Okay. So when we goin'?" Lorenzo asked.

"Right now. Let's squad up," I instructed.

"We goin' heavy this time?" Sayeed asked.

"Not extremely, but definitely not as light as last time. Renzo, have Jo Jo and them meet us on 134th and Guy Brewer in a half hour," I instructed as Lorenzo pulled out his cell and began to text.

"I'll go pull the truck around," Sayeed added.

"Cool. Listen Shanise. I'm gonna need you to sit this one out. Shit might get a lil' funky and…"

"Nigga please. Let's go," she said cutting me off and sashaying passed me.

After meeting with Jo Jo and the boys on 134th Ave, and instructing them on how to handle the upcoming situation, we convoyed five cars deep a few blocks up to Baisley Projects. When we pulled up on the block, Bruno was in plain sight and damn near in the same spot as before. A few soldiers and a couple of chicks surrounded him. I shook my head as I counted more chicks than niggas. That was definitely a young boy slip move. As usual, we cocked our weapons as we pulled up. Bruno and his boys pulled their weapons but put them away when they saw it was me. That would be slip move number two. All cars in my convoy emptied its passengers as I approached Bruno and took a mental picture of the surprised look on his face as he spoke.

"Nigga you almost got ya ass sho…"

I swiftly pulled my pistol smacked him across the face. The girls scattered and the few soldiers he had with him wanted to reach but noticed that they were heavily outmanned and outgunned so they thought better of it. I stood over Bruno with my barrel pointed in his face, as blood leaked from his mouth and nose.

"Do I bleed once a month motherfucker?"

"What?" he said grimacing in pain.

"Do I look like a pussy?" I said as I delivered a kick to his rib cage.

"Yo Tray you buggin' fam. What's all this about?"

"Don't play dumb motherfucker. We both know what this is about. The sooner you realize that I own this city and you just rent space from me, the better off you will be. I see and hear everything motherfucker. Now the question is, does this little disagreement alter our business arrangement or do I have to cut off your lifeline and shut this whole operation down out here?"

He hesitated and screwed up his face in anger. I put one in the chamber and put my foot on his chest.

"I'll ask one more time. Do we have a problem? If we do, then we might as well solve it right now."

His eyes scanned the immediate area for his soldiers, a good samaritan, or any sign of help, but there was none so he had to comply.

"We Gucci my nigga, everything is cool. Let's get this money my gee."

With that being said, I helped his bitch ass to his feet and to add insult to injury, I patted him on top of his head.

"It's gonna be a'ight son. From now on let's just have a lot more grip and a lot less lip. Let's ride out ya'll."

My team got back in our vehicles with smirks on our faces, while Bruno and his team looked the total opposite. Maybe I went too far by embarrassing and clowning Bruno in front of his entire neighborhood, but it was a necessary evil and it needed to be done. I didn't anticipate any retaliation from Bruno, I was his money tree and without money he was nothing.

W.T.F ???

Things were still really rocky at home with me and Janelle, so I decided to check into a suite for a few days. The truth of the matter is things had been rocky for years. I realized a long time ago that she was only still around for the money and she realized I was only still around for the kids. I would have divorced her years ago if she didn't know so much about me. There is nothing worse than a woman scorned.

"Baby what's wrong? You seem so distant," Sophia said as she lay across my chest.

"My bad baby. I just got a lot on my mind," I replied staring up at the ceiling.

"I'm not just talking about today. You haven't been the same since you sent me to get Tiffany out. I thought you would be relieved after you totally fucked her life up."

I had met Sophia a little over three years ago, when she walked into the club one day after work. I remember it like it was yesterday. She had on a tight form fitting grey skirt suit, her hair was pulled up into a bun and she had on black blouse, diamond watch and a matching tennis bracelet. The skirt accentuated her perfectly shaped ass that protruded through the material and her thirty-eight double D's had the exact same effect on her blouse. She was carrying a Louis Vuitton briefcase as she sat at the bar and ordered a Cirroc and pineapple juice. I couldn't help myself, I had to walk over and make a move. I introduced myself and she was a little standoffish at first, but persistence overcame resistance and within a few minutes we were talking like old friends. She told me that she was a defense attorney and I told her that I owned the club. After talking like what seemed like forever, we exchanged numbers and hit it off great. She told me that she was originally from Jacksonville, Florida and although she was in the legal field, she had strong ties to the streets because her brothers and her father ran Duvall County with an iron fist. She knew the street life like the back of her hand and only got into law because her father wanted more for his baby girl, so he sent her to Columbia University and footed the bill. After graduating at the top of her class, she got a job at one of the top law firms in NYC so she decided to stay. When I heard that her story was so similar to mines it bugged me out. We started spending major time together and getting really close to each other. I had learned about holding back from my past mistakes with Tiffany so I decided to keep it one hundred with her and tell her about Shanise and the kids and the crazy shit is, she was so thorough she didn't even care.

I found venting to Sophia to be very therapeutic, and the fact that she welcomed it made it easier to open up to her. It made it so easy that I decided to go all in and tell her everything, about Horse, about D-Boy, about Tiffany, about everything. However, before I confided all of this information into her, I retained her services as my attorney. I did this for two reasons, number one, she had close ties to the D.A.'s office which meant that I had an inside plug whenever some shit was coming down against me and that allowed me to be proactive and dance around it. And most importantly, with Sophia being my attorney I was protected by attorney/client privilege, which meant by law I could tell her anything and there would be nothing she could ever do about it. Besides, we had developed a special love for one another. She had become the Bonnie to my Clyde. She watched me do dirt and even told me how to legally get out of some shit. Sophia had become the type of rider that I know Tiffany would have been if I would have only kept it real with her. I can't erase what I did to her, but I could make it right, which is why I doctored the documents and drummed up the story about the records being found in D-Boy's crib. See, having Sophia in my corner and in my bed allowed me to manipulate the system, and now that I was able to have Tiffany freed, my conscience would be clear, but it wasn't my conscience I was worried about.

"Look. I just don't know if getting Tiffany out was a good idea. How can we be sure that she's not gonna come around looking for trouble?"

"Trust me Travon, I put the fear of God in that bitch. She thinks you'll kill her if she comes anywhere near you. I'm telling you, she's just happy to be free. I can assure you, she is not even thinking about you."

"Yeah well I hope you're right."

MASTERPLAN

I had been contemplating how to handle this Travon situation. I had no idea of what I wanted to do but I knew I wanted to do something and I was getting no help from Monica. Every time I tried to talk to her about it she gave me a million and one reasons to leave him alone. Truth be told, she was pissing me the fuck off. So I decided to take matters into my own hands. I called Michelle and set up another meeting, this time the meeting was at the Hard Rock Café down at the harbor and this time I beat her to the meeting place.

"Hey girl what's up?" I said as she approached the booth I had reserved for us.

"Ain't shit. I was surprised you called back. I ain't heard from you since I gave you that info on your ex," she said sitting down.

"I know girl, I just been soaking it all in and trying to put everything into perspective."

"I can dig it. So what did you come up with?"

"Well I kicked a few ideas around in my head and they all revolved around you."

"Around me?" she said sounding surprised.

"Yes you. How close are you with this dude that despises Travon so much?"

"Girl I got that nigga wrapped around my finger twice. I done been up there like five or six times since the last time we spoke, it be at his request too. I got the nigga sprung all crazy. He keeps asking me to move up there. He said he would get me a crib and everything and I was about to jump on it but after hearing your story, I was like nah, I'm good."

I must have screwed up my face at that last sentence because she immediately tried to fix it.

"Oh shit babe. I didn't mean anything by that," she said apologetically.

"Nah, it's cool. I'm glad you could learn from my fuck up. So does this dude hate Travon enough to make a move on him?" I asked looking for an angle.

"At first I would say yes. But I was there the other day and saw Travon punk the shit out of him and he ain't do shit."

"Word?"

"Giiiiirl, pistol whipped him and everything. I was like *oh shit it's about to go down*, but it never did."

"Get the fuck outta here. He just let that shit ride?" I said shocked at the news because Travon never showed this violent side to me.

"After Travon left, we went back to my hotel and I patched him up. He was talkin' that *watch that nigga gonna get his shit.* But I doubt he did shit."

"He's our way in," I said snapping my fingers.

"What do you mean?" she asked with a perplexed look on her face.

"I'm not sure yet, but somehow, someway, we gotta use you and Bruno's connection along with his hatred for Travon to sting the shit out of this motherfucker. The question is, are you with me on this?" I asked looking her square in the eye.

"Of course I am, you think I forgot how you took care of me while I was in lock up? I told you then that I would always have your back no matter what and I meant that baby, so any and everything you need you can count me in."

"Okay Chelle, but I warn you, if you cross me you can give your soul to God because your ass belongs to me," I said sternly.

"Never that baby. I got you."

"Okay cool. Give me a few days to get a plan together and I'll be in touch. Your job is to keep that nigga Bruno on the hook for as long as possible at all costs."

"Oh trust me. That nigga ain't going nowhere. He's all in for this pussy."

"Okay well keep it that way. I gotta get going. I got some things to put together."

I got up, gave her a kiss and left. Once I hit the highway I was once again lost in my own thoughts. I had a million and one scenarios on how to handle this Travon shit and the most simplest was to have somehow put the battery in Bruno's back just enough to have him push Travon's wig back. Then I thought to myself *damn, he got a wife and kids.* The thought was quickly erased as I remembered I was supposed to be his wife, and he indirectly killed our kid, so as far as I was concerned everything and everyone was fair game. As I pulled up to the stoplight, I inadvertently caught a glimpse of myself in the rear view mirror and saw a reflection of a woman, the woman wasn't me but I liked her and I liked what she stood for. So it was time to become her. When the light turned green, I made a beeline straight for the beauty supply store. It was time for me to become the woman I saw in the mirror and I vowed to play the part well.

A few hours later I emerged from my bathroom in my robe and a towel wrapped around my head. When I got home Monica wasn't there, but now here she was sitting on my bed.

"Hey Tiff what's up?" she asked as she sat with one leg folded underneath her.

"Everything is good girl. Everything is all good," I responded as I sprayed myself with some Flower Bomb.

"So listen. I have this friend who wants to take me out tonight and he has a friend. They are both Senior Brokers at their firm, so you know they got them deep pockets," she said with a devilish grin.

"No girl. Not again. I'm good. I got a lot on my mind so I think I'm just gonna chill and watch a movie or something," I said declining the offer.

"What? Girl you ain't really did shit since you been home."

"That's because I got a lot of shit going on. You think just because I'm free that everything is all good, but I'm still traumatized. You forget that I lost four years of my life. That's something you just don't bounce back from after a few months. I appreciate the offer, but a nigga is the last thing on my mind right now."

"Okay girl. Suit ya' self, but you know you can't carry that shit forever. You gonna have to shake it sooner or later. It's time for you to put that shit behind you. It's time to re-introduce yourself to the world."

"Oh I'm already on that. Voila'." I said as I removed that towel from my head, showing my new cut and styled honey blonde doo."

"Oh shit. Check you out. That shit is hot as hell. When did you do that?" she asked admiring the new me.

"This is what I been doing for the past couple of hours. I figured I needed a change if I was gonna start fresh."

"That's what's up. Girl I'm so glad you decided to leave that Travon shit alone," she said with a sigh of relief.

"See. That's where you're wrong. On the contrary, the plan to go after Travon is still in effect. I met with Michelle again today to double check her story and after careful consideration I have decided that I will never be able to get a fresh start until that nigga is dealt with, so as soon as I connect a few more dots it's game time. Are you ready?" I asked raising my hand for a high five.

"Yeah Tiffany. I'm with you," she said ignoring my high five and walking out of the room. Something wasn't right with her, but I just couldn't put my finger on it. But one thing's for sure, the shit didn't sit well with me at all.

GETTING THE BALL ROLLING

Over the next month or so, I racked my brains crazy trying to think of a plan to put into action and after all that thinking, I decided that I needed to get up close and personal and observe the situation myself. If I was going to risk my life and freedom, I needed to be more hands on with the situation, so I told Michelle that on her next trip to New York that I would come with her. Strangely enough, even though I insisted Monica stay home because I wasn't feeling her vibe, she insisted on coming and that we should all ride in her car. She was really starting to weird me out with her actions, but I let it ride out. Michelle had called ahead to inform Bruno that she was bringing some friends and to have a suite waiting for us. He must really be a trick nigga because he still offered to fly all three of us up to New York, but still, Monica insisted on us driving up in her car and as soon as we picked Michelle up, her reasons were evident. We pulled up and Michelle was already on the porch waiting. She put her bags in the trunk and got in the back seat.

"Hey girl you ready?" she asked excited about the road trip.

"Excuse me. Do you normally get in peoples cars without introducing yourself or acknowledging them?" Monica barked going right in on her.

Michelle was so shocked at the outburst that her mouth just hung open, so I jumped in to save her.

"Oh my bad, Monica this is Michelle."

"Hey nice to meet you," Michelle said hesitantly extending her hand.

"Yeah. I know who you are. You the broad that don't mind her business and got my girl all gung ho to go out and fuck her life up again and possibly get herself killed. You about a simple bitch," Monica spat through the rear view mirror, totally disrespecting Michelle.

I had heard enough.

"Yo Monica chill he fuck out. I don't know what's gotten into you lately but you been seriously tripping. Now we got a long ass ride and an even longer stay in New York, so if you gonna be on ya' motherfucking period the whole time, then you can keep ya' motherfucking ass in Maryland," I snapped.

"Nah, I'm coming. Somebody gotta keep ya'll dumb bitches from getting ya 'self's killed."

"Tiff, I went ahead and made you a driver's license under an alias name. You never know if or when it may come in handy, especially in New York. This is one of my best pieces of work, so don't say I ain't never did nothing for your ass" Michelle joked handing me the license."

"Thanks Chelle. I really appreciate you looking out for me," I responded with a smile on my face despite still being pissed about Monica's nasty behavior towards Michelle.

It was a long and quiet trip to New York but once we got through the Holland Tunnel and entered Manhattan, I immediately felt two things. I felt my blood boiling and I felt a feeling of vindication. Even though I still didn't have a game plan, I could smell vengeance in the air and something told me that things would work themselves out.

We pulled up to the valet at the W Hotel in midtown Manhattan. Apparently Bruno had made reservations for us there. The valet took the keys to the car, the bellboy took our bags and we entered the hotel. Michelle went to check us in since the reservations were in her name, while me and Monica sat in the waiting area of the lobby.

"Okay. You got us here now what?" Monica asked sarcastically.

"Look Monica, I don't know yet okay? If you gave more input instead of being so fucking negative about the situation maybe we could come up with something together," I responded in a mono toned voice.

"Well Tiffany, what do you want me to do, just sit back and watch you put yourself in danger? You play this shit the wrong way and no doubt about it Travon will kill you, I guarantee it."

"How can you guarantee anything Mon...."

We were interrupted by Michelle's happy ass.

97

"Here you go ladies," she said as she handed us the keys to the room.

We took the keys and headed towards the elevators. Monica pushed the button for the 29th floor. We rode the elevator in silence until we reached our destination. The doors opened and we scanned the sign on the wall for room 2903. It directed us to make a left, so that's where we headed. About halfway down the hall Monica and I stopped in front of our door while Michelle continued to walk.

"It's right here Michelle," I said trying to stop her.

"Naw babe. Ya'll are in 2903. I'm in 2905. You know I can't be getting dicked down with ya'll in the same room, but don't worry, I'll be right next door if you need me," she said with a wink as she entered her room.

I smiled at the comment while Monica rolled her eyes and opened our door. As it turned out our room was a two-bedroom luxury suite filled with lavish amenities. I mean, for all intensive purposes, it looked like a moderate sized apartment. Well one thing was for sure, Michelle ain't lie, this nigga Bruno did it big and he was eating lovely off of Travon. I had to meet this nigga to see exactly how I could use him as a pawn to fuck Travon's life up. It wasn't gonna be easy, but I didn't care. At this point, I was all in.

I woke up from a well-needed nap after that long ass drive, but now I was ready to get down to business. I was starving and decided to see if Monica wanted to grab something to eat. I figured we would stuff our faces and see what New York had to offer so that I could get my mind off of Travon's bitch ass for a minute. I went to her room and knocked, when I didn't get an answer I opened the door and saw that she wasn't there. I figured she might be in the living room since I heard the television, but she wasn't in there either. I thought to myself *damn this bitch could've at least let me know she was leaving.* Well I wasn't gonna let that ruin my night. I took a nice hot shower, threw on my BCBG sweat suit and white Jordans and headed next door to Michelle's room to see what she was up to.

I knocked on the door and thought Michelle's ass had dipped out too until the door finally opened and there stood the finest light skinned nigga I had seen since meeting T.I. a few years back.

"What up?" he said eyeing the way my body filled out my sweat suit and the way my cleavage spilled out of the top.

"How you doing? My name is Tiffany. Is Michelle around?" I asked eye fucking him back. I was never really into street guys, but this dude had an arrogance about him that instantly turned me on. Or maybe it was just the fact that it had been years since I had been this close to a man. Either way, the fitted jeans, wife beater over the six-pack and dark piercing eyes made me stare a bit longer than I wanted to.

"Yeah Michelle's in the shower, but you can come in and chill until she gets out if you want."

I walked passed him leaving a trail of my Gucci Guilty perfume as I stepped down into the sunken living room and took a seat on the leather sectional. I subconsciously took in the beauty of the suite, from the white marble flooring, the expensive chandeliers hanging from the cathedral ceilings to the artwork that was artistically placed throughout the suite. This suite was twice the size of the one Monica and I was staying in, and could easily be pictured on the cover of any of those magazines that featured high-end accommodations throughout the city. The best part of the suite had to be the breathtaking view of the New York City skyline that lit up through the floor to ceiling window in the living room. Bruno walked over to the bar and fixed himself a shot of Patron.

"Um. Can I fix you a drink Ma?" he asked.

"No thanks. I haven't eaten anything all day so that wouldn't be a good idea," I said as I got up and walked over to the picturesque window to take in the view of the city.

"Damn I thought the suite you got for me and Monica was hot, but this shit right here is crazy. Don't get me wrong; we really appreciate you footing the bill for our weekend getaway. I don't want you to think that I'm ungrateful," I said still admiring the view.

"Now why would I think something like that Tiffany? To be honest, you look like you're use to the finer things in life, so I'm glad I can maintain to your standards," Bruno responded digging deep.

I admit I enjoyed the attention he was giving me; it had been a while since I allowed myself to relax and not let the thoughts of getting payback on Travon consume my every being.

"Hey girl. What you doing here?" Michelle asked as she entered the living room wearing nothing but a white robe, while drying her wet hair.

"I came by to see what was up for tonight, I was initially gonna hang with Monica because I figured you would be busy, but when I woke up her ass was nowhere to be found so I figured I would come over here and see what was up with you," I responded finally turning away from the window.

"Oh so I was ya second choice bitch? Anyway me and Bruno just finished some personal business," Michelle said grinning from ear to ear.

"TMI. Don't nobody wanna hear about you and Bruno's nasty assess getting it in. My ass is hungry and bored so I need you to get dressed. I ain't trying to sit up in no hotel all night and I especially ain't tryna be no third wheel with you and Bruno."

"Yo. Ya'll chicks are funny. I would love to show you beautiful ladies around the city, unfortunately me and my boys got some business to take care of tonight. I'm about to head out, but Michelle let me know if ya'll are interested in hanging out after you get ya girls stomach right. We probably gonna hit a club after we done so I'll text you the info, put ya'll on the V.I.P. list and send a limo service through to pick ya'll up so you don't have to worry about navigating your way through the city," Bruno said putting his shirt on and grabbing his keys.

"Okay Bae, I'll let you know what we decide to do. You always know how to take care of me when I come to town." Michelle said, as she walked over and slid her tongue into his mouth, and then she walked him to the door and did it again.

"A'ight Tiff. I'll see you later," he said with that oooh I can't wait to fuck you face.

"Same here," I said playing his game as Michelle closed the door.

"Okay let me throw something on. I'm kind of hungry too," she said speed walking into the bedroom.

Let the games begin.

DISAPPEARING ACT

"Monica are you sure Tiffany has no idea where you are?"

"No baby, I told you that when I left the suite she was sound asleep. I even went as far as to stand over her and gently call her name, but she was dead to the world. I also just checked my cell and she hasn't called me at all so maybe she's still asleep, or knowing Tiffany, she is out somewhere sipping on some pretty colorful drink."

"Okay Monica. I don't need you fucking up our plans. We came too far to have shit backfire on us now. As a matter of fact, I don't know why you couldn't just keep her fucking ass out of New York in the first place."

"Baby I told you I tried, but Tiffany is all gung ho since that chick Michelle put that bug in her ear, but don't worry, we're only here for the weekend. I'm going to try my best to keep her out of the way as much as possible. If we do head out, I'll make sure we do some tourist things like Central Park, eating at some of those nice outdoor restaurants, and of course a shit load of shopping. We won't be in your neck of the woods, so let's just get through the weekend with no arguments. Trust me baby, I know how to play my position and I know everything that is at risk, but the truth of the matter is I don't know how much longer I can stay away from you. You promised that once Tiffany was free, you and I were going to jet off and live a nice quiet life together. I need a break from all this stress, lying to my best friend is not as easy as you think. Now you go and switch up the plan, and I'm trying my hardest to be there to support you. I know how important this is to us, but remember Tiffany has more street smarts now than she did before."

"Look Monica. I hear all that shit you saying, but you and me ain't going nowhere until I finish what I started. I know Tiffany is your girl, but right now you gonna have to choose a side. Don't start getting cold feet on me now. Trust me, in the end, this is all gonna be worth it."

"Okay baby. I trust you. Now let me get up and take a quick shower, and head back to the hotel. Hopefully I can slip back in without Tiffany asking me twenty one questions."

"Okay Monica. I got a lot of shit to do today so I gotta head out, lock the door behind you when you leave."

"Okay baby. I love you and please be careful out there."

"Always."

TANGLED WEBS

"Damn that steak and lobster tail was on point," I said while rubbing my stomach."

"Yeah, I have no complaints about the glazed salmon. It was cooked to perfection," Michelle said kissing her fingers Italian style.

We had decided to order room service because we didn't want to leave since Monica was still missing in action.

"I'm still pissed that Monica didn't even have the decency to call or leave a note or anything," I said.

"Don't worry Tiff. I'm sure she went out shopping or something and just lost track of time. That happens a lot out here. She can handle herself and will probably be back soon."

"Yeah well she needs to hurry the hell up. I wanna get out and enjoy myself," I said getting antsy.

"Well if you want I can call Bruno and tell him to put us on the V.I.P. list so we can hang out for a few hours."

"Thanks Chelle, but let's wait for Monica's ass to surface before we decide what to get into tonight."

And just then, on queue Monica walked in with a few Bergdorf Goodman bags in her hands.

"Hey Chicas. What ya'll bitches up to?" she said all giddy and shit.

"Uh uh. Where the hell you been?" I asked a little pissed off.

"Oh I went out and did a little shopping. I tried to wake you but you was out for the count."

"You ain't try that damn hard to wake me up, and why didn't you leave a damn note or something?"

"Uh. Last time I checked, my mother gave up her parental rights when I was fifteen. What the fuck is you tripping for?"

"Monica, Tiff was just worried about you that's all. Ain't no need for ya'll to be fighting and shit. Let's just enjoy the time we have here," Michelle interjected trying to keep the peace.

"You know what Michelle. That's the first thing yo ass said that I agree with. I guess you do make sense sometimes," Monica replied.

"Oh whatever bitch shut up," I joked.

"Look okay. You're right. I should have left a note or something. I'm sorry mommy. If I let you spank me will you forgive me?" Monica said with a flirtatious grin.

"No time for that. We are painting the town red tonight," I replied informing her of the night's events.

"What? Going out? Not me, I'm beat. Ya'll go right on ahead without me. I'm gonna lay it down," Monica said yawning.

"Oh hell no. Your ass dipped out all day solo, now you wanna stay home? Negative, get ya ass dressed," I instructed with a firmness that showed I meant business.

"Well look, ya'll figure it out while I go get freshened up and throw some hot shit on. Toodles bitches," Michelle said as she left the suite.

"Look Monica, I'm getting in the shower and I suggest you do the same thing so when I get out you should be getting ready," I instructed.

"Okay Tiff. Damn. I'm about to get in the shower too."

"Good." I responded as I headed for the shower in my room.

I was in the shower as my mind raced a million miles per minute. I was still not sure how this would play out. Shit, for all I know I could be face to face with Travon before the night was over and then what would I do. Maybe Monica was right. Maybe I should just stay out of his way and try to start life over. I was so confused and mentally fucked up; I had no idea what to do. I decided to leave it in God's hands. He had brought me too far to drop me off and leave me stranded. So fuck it. Let's roll the dice, I thought to myself, as I got out of the shower, grabbed a towel and opened the door to my room only to find Monica sprawled across my bed with nothing but a towel on. I sat down and began to apply my lotion.

"Girl ain't you supposed to be getting ready?" I asked not looking over at her.

"Hey. I was thinking. Maybe we could just stay in tonight," she said rubbing my shoulders.

"What? Girl we already been through this, now I said we..."

She cut me off by grabbing my face and sliding her tongue into my mouth. I was almost entrapped in the moment, but then quickly came to my senses and pulled away from her.

"Hold up Monica. Why the sudden change of heart? I recall trying to give you some of these goodies when I got home and you straight shitted on me. Now you come out of nowhere and wanna get it in. Nah, I'm cool. Besides, I need to stay focused on the task at hand. Now get dressed, ain't no telling' when that limo is gonna be here," I said probably shattering her ego.

"Tiffany, you are just doing something to me tonight shorty. I need to taste that, we can stay in and fuck all crazy," she said as she attempted to undo my towel.

"Move Monica. Ain't nobody playing with yo ass. Now I said stop and I meant it," I responded getting up. Now her ego was totally broken I was sure.

"Yeah a'ight. Whatever yo," she said as she stormed out of the room like a little kid.

I let out a big deep sigh and proceeded to get back on my square.

NOW WE'RE GETTING SOMEWHERE

When the Limo pulled up in front of the club, the line was around the corner, but Michelle had called ahead to let Bruno know we were getting close so he had the bouncer waiting to escort us through the red velvet rope which allowed us to skip the line and walk right in. The club was nice and the music was banging. I loved New York DJ's, they knew how to play that hot shit. The bouncer escorted us through the club to the glass encased V.I.P. section where Bruno was waiting at a table alone with about seven or eight bottles of top shelf liquor and champagne.

"What's good ladies?" he said without standing. Showing he had no couth whatsoever.

"Hey baby," Michelle screamed, running to him like a little puppy dog, or like she ain't just fuck this nigga a few hours ago.

She hugged him and went to kiss him on the mouth, but he turned his cheek to her and this hoe didn't even check him on it.

"Okay so I have already had the pleasure of meeting you Tiffany. I'm glad you came out tonight. And who are you?" he asked Monica as he grabbed her hand and attempted to kiss it before she snatched it back.

"Move nigga. I don't know where ya mouth been," she snapped coldly.

"Baby this is Tiffany's friend Monica," Michelle said making sure to point out that she didn't really fuck with Monica all too tough.

"Hey Monica. How you doin'? They call me Young Bruno."

"Young huh? Figures," Monica responded still giving him her ass to kiss.

"Okay I see somebody is a little grumpy from the long drive. Well it's all good. Ya'll are my guests tonight so anything you want, don't hesitate to ask. Money is definitely not an issue so make yourselves comfortable and enjoy the night," Bruno said still trying to be polite.

"So where are your boys at?" I asked noticing that he was sitting there alone.

"Oh they scattered around. They can see me and I can see them. That's what's important," he responded.

"So why they ain't up here with you?" I asked being nosey.

"Everything ain't for everybody. I don't allow everyone to get close to me, then they get comfortable and forget what they role is."

"Damn I respect that a hundred percent," I responded stroking his ego.

"Well I'm glad you do."

"So you gonna look like the man poppin' bottles with three bad bitches in V.I.P. all by yourself huh? Is that how you get down?" I continued.

"That's exactly how I get down. Nothing but the finest things in life for me."

"Yeah well that makes two of us," I said with a flirtatious smile.

"So baby, did you miss me," Michelle said stepping in between Bruno and me.

The look on his face said that he didn't approve of that move.

"You already know I did, and when we finished partying, I'm coming back to your hotel and drop something off in ya drawers."

"I think I just threw up in my mouth," Monica spat out.

"Damn Ma. What you trippin' for?" Bruno responded no longer able to conceal his agitation.

"Nigga ain't nobody tripping. You said spare no expense right? Excuse me waiter, can I have the filet mignon, medium well with twin rock lobster tails, a side salad with blue cheese dressing, oh and two Magnums of Ace of Spades," Monica said as she waved down a passing waiter.

The waiter looked at Bruno for his approval and as bad as he wanted to tell Monica to go fuck herself, she had called his bluff so shutting down her order would mean she had won. He asked Michelle and I if we wanted anything and we declined. He painfully gave the waiter the okay.

"So Mr. Bruno, I heard a lot about you," I said starting back up.

"Oh yeah? What you heard about me?"

"My girl tells me that you the man out here and you got New York on lock. She makes it sound like you got the whole city bowing down to you and kneeling at your feet," I continued gassing him up.

"Yeah well she ain't lie to you," Bruno replied lying through his teeth.

"Hmm. Well no wonder my girl Chelle is stuck to you like glue."

"That's right. This is my boo ski," Michelle jumped in throwing her arms around Bruno, seeming to try and fuck up my plans

"Yo. What's up with your friend?" Bruno said ignoring Michelle and referring to Monica who was sitting at a table alone and had been texting the whole time.

"Oh Monica just gotta get to know you," I said trying to defend her rudeness.

"Yeah boo. She is nowhere near as friendly as Tiffany is," Michelle chimed in apparently coming at my neck.

Although Bruno wasn't sharp enough to catch the insult, I shot Michelle a look that told her if she didn't cut it out, I would whip her ass where she stood.

"Well in any event, there is plenty food and liquor so let's get this party started," Bruno said, popping open a bottle of Ace Of Spades."

And that's exactly what we did. We drank, danced and partied like it was our last day on earth. I was even able to soften Monica up a little bit and get her on the dance floor. Bruno spared no expense at trying to make a great impression on us, and he was doing a good job.

When the club was over, and it was time to head back to the hotel; Bruno insisted on driving us back to the hotel as opposed to us having the car service take us back. The whole ride back he openly flirted with all of us, and we each took it a different way. I looked at it as a way to get closer to him. Michelle seemed a little aggravated and Monica was back on her bullshit and texting on her phone the whole time.

When we arrived at the hotel, we piled out of Bruno's truck and headed for the entrance, all of us except Monica who headed towards the valet parking lot.

"Uhhh and where do you think you are going?" I asked.

"I'm going to tend to my business thank you," she joked while opening her car door.

"Bitch it's almost 5:30 in the morning. What type of business you got in New York this time of morning?"

"My business, now mind yours. Nighty night Tiff," she said as she closed her car door and pulled off.

Me, Michelle, and Bruno got off the elevator on our floor and proceeded down the hall towards our suites. I stopped in front of mines.

"Okay ya'll have fun," I said yawning as I dug through my purse looking for my room key.

"You know we will girl," Michelle said hanging all over Bruno.

"Hold up. You calling it a night already?" Bruno said licking his lips LL Cool J style.

"Hell yeah. These shoes are killing my feet. I just wanna soak in the Jacuzzi and lay in my bed," I responded meaning every word of it.

"Well we got a Jacuzzi over here and its way bigger than the one in your suite, so you can come over here and take a load off and just chill for a while," he responded not giving up.

I was just about to decline his offer when I saw Michelle's green ass roll her eyes. I wondered what her problem was.

"Okay, Okay. But only for a little while," I responded pretending to not really want to go.

Michelle rolled her eyes once again. Oooh I couldn't wait to get that bitch alone and straighten her ass out. I walked right passed her as Bruno opened the door while keeping his eyes glued to me.

Once inside the suite, Bruno got right down to business by unlocking the V.I.P. bar and popping open a bottle of Dom Perignon. He then grabbed three champagne flutes and made his way to the kitchen island and filled them up.

"Here you go ladies," he said as he gently slid two glasses down the breakfast bar.

"No thanks. I'm good. It's going on six in the morning and I'm tired as hell," I responded pushing the drink back.

"Aww come on. I got plenty of shit to keep you up," he said pulling bags out of his pocket that contained weed, coke, and ecstasy. This dude was a walking felony.

I still declined, but surprisingly Michelle dove right in.

"That's what I'm talking about baby. Pass me one of them skittles," she said referring to the pills.

"Yeah Chelle, I knew you wouldn't break tradition," Bruno replied inferring that he and Chelle did this during her visits.

If I was going to get close to this nigga, I couldn't let him think that I was some square broad so I had to do something.

"It ain't that I'm judging or nothing, but I don't need none of that shit to party. Like I said, my feet and my body are killing me."

"Yeah you did say that right? Michelle go run the Jacuzzi and use some of the bath beads and oils under the sink," he instructed while never taking his eyes off of me.

"Excuse me?" Michelle responded showing her agitation at the command.

"Yo, you heard me. Run the fucking water and we'll be in there in a minute," he re-iterated a bit more firm this time as Michelle rolled her eyes and left to do as she was told.

I took my heels off and started rubbing my feet and Bruno wasted no time going right in on me.

"You shouldn't be doin' that yourself. Come over here and let me handle that for you," he said patting the sofa.

"Nah I'm cool. But thanks anyway," I said stringing him along.

"Look Ma. If you worried about Michelle, don't be, this ain't her first time around the block with me. She already knows what it's hitting for."

I grabbed the bottle of champagne and headed over to the sofa. I could tell I was gonna need it for the mornings events. I sat down and Bruno put my right leg on his lap and started massaging my foot.

"Damn that feels good," I moaned meaning every word of it.

"Yeah. I've been told that I am nice with my hands," he replied being cocky.

"Hmm, Is that a fact?" I asked dangling the carrot in front of the jackass.

"Hell yeah and there's plenty more where that came from."

"That's what they all say."

Then without warning he leaned over and started kissing me. I started to resist and then thought *this is gonna be easier than I thought,* so I grabbed his head and passionately kissed him back. It had been so long since I kissed a man that I forgot that I was acting for a minute. I was lost in my own fantasy as I imagined that Bruno was not the ill-mannered, womanizing, drug dealing thug that he was, instead he was my tall, dark, knight in shining armor that would swoop in and take me away from this madness and end this nightmare, but he wasn't he was Bruno. He was rough as his hands went up my dress and snatched my thongs off, but I didn't care. I needed the touch of a man and at this point any man would do. He fingered my tight pussy feverishly as I bit into his neck to brace myself for the guilty pleasures he was bringing me.

"Yeah bitch. You like that shit, don't you?" he asked feeling himself just as much as he was feeling me. He had fucked up the fantasy, now it was time to win my academy award.

"Yes daddy. I wanted this since the first time I saw you baby," I lied convincingly.

"Yeah I fuckin' knew it. You want this dick don't you?"

I never got a chance to lie again.

"Hey babe, I can't find the ..." Michelle said as she walked in on us.

"Yo. What the fuck is going on? She asked obviously not feeling what she was seeing.

"Chelle stop trippin' like we ain't never did this before," Bruno said annoyed at the interruption.

"Yeah Bruno, but this is my fucking friend, or at least I thought she was," Michelle snapped, shooting me a piercing look as Bruno's phone rang.

"I gotta get this. Ya'll bitches figure this shit out," he said as he left the room.

When I was sure he was gone and out of earshot, I let loose on Michelle.

"What the fuck is wrong with you?" I barked in a loud whisper.

"I don't know Tiffany. I think I'm really feeling him," she responded

"Well un-fucking feel him. You knew what this was from day one. Now is there gonna be an issue with you playing your part? If so, let me know now so I will know what I'm dealing with."

"Okay Tiff, I'm all in. I'm sorry baby. I don't know what came over me, but it's your show. You run it how you see fit."

"That's good to hear. Now let's just get through this visit with no problems and then work on planning the next one. I'm not gonna rest until Travon is in a cell or in a box, I put that on my mom and dad."

"Well like I said, I'm with you, but ya girl Monica be actin' real funny style. You sure she good money?"

"What? Bitch don't you ever question the loyalty my girl got for me. Do not get it twisted Michelle, you the fucking outsider," I said sternly pointing in her face.

Her words stung, but she was one hundred percent right. Monica had been acting very funny.

"I know Tiffany. I'm just hoping that your friendship with her ain't blinding you."

It was then that Bruno made his way back into the room.

"Ya'll hoes got ya'll mind right yet?" he asked disrespectfully.

"Yeah daddy everything is everything," I said as I grabbed Michelle and stuck my tongue in her mouth.

LAST DAYS

I woke up in between Bruno and Michelle. All three of us naked as the day we were born. Two empty bottles of Dom Perignon stared at me from the nigh stand. The bag that once contained the ecstasy was spilled out, there was coke on a mirror and the room smelled like a weed house, and although I know I didn't indulge in the drugs, the room was spinning like a carnival ride. I tried to move, but my head and my pussy were both hurting like hell. I mustered up the energy to climb over Michelle who along with Bruno was dead to the world. I gathered my belongings and headed next door to my own suite to wash the filth and grime from the morning sexcapade away.

When I opened the door to my suite, I headed straight for my bedroom. On the way, I stopped to see if Monica was back, it was 10:46am and I had not heard from her since she left earlier, but she was not there. Oh well, I was too tired and aggravated to give a fuck. I threw my clothes off and jumped into the shower. I scrubbed so hard it felt like I was scraping my skin off. I scrubbed as if I could scrub away the memory of what I had just done, but who was I fooling? It was a done deal, and no amount of soap would take it away. My only hope now, was that I had performed well enough both mentally, and sexually to get a request for an encore performance. When I got out of the shower I headed back into my room, lotioned my skin and slipped on my cami. I climbed into bed and cried myself to sleep, as I felt myself sinking deeper and deeper into a situation that I prayed that I would make it out of.

I was awakened by the sound of the suite door slamming shut. I jumped up and looked at the clock and saw that it was now almost 2pm. I put on my slippers and went to see why Monica was slamming shit. I found her in the living room sitting on the couch.

"Welcome back Houdini," I said sarcastically joking.

"Bitch, don't start. I am not in the mood."

"Uh Uh. Don't be coming up in here fucking up our last day in New York with that bad ass attitude."

"Whatever. Look Tiffany, I'm tired and I just wanna go to bed."

"What crawled up your ass and died?"

"Well for starters, you had me hanging out all night with that lame ass nigga Bruno. Then I went to see my friend and...look I just wanna go to bed okay."

"Okay well don't be trying to sleep all day. Like I said, this our last day, and I ain't tryna waste it waiting for you to get up."

"Man fuck all that shit. This whole trip was a fucking waste of time."

"What?"

"Yeah. What the fuck did you accomplish? You met one of Travon's flunkies. Big fucking deal. Now what Sherlock? Where's this big elaborate plan?"

"It's coming together." I lied, trying to defend myself.

"Fuck outta here. You ain't put shit together. You ain't built for this shit. Now take the lesson on the chin and put it behind you already. I'm going the fuck to bed. I did my part by coming out here with your crazy ass. Now it's over," Monica said as she stormed off and slammed her bedroom door.

She left me speechless. I had no comeback whatsoever to her ranting. Maybe she was right. I mean, besides partying and fucking Bruno, what else did I accomplish this weekend? I was suddenly overcome with the urge to cut the trip short and head back to Maryland. I dare mention it to Monica; I figured I would let her sleep off her attitude. I went next door to see if Chelle was up but I got no answer when I knocked on her door. *Ugghhhh!* I thought to myself, as I headed back to my suite.

I plopped down on the couch and flipped through the channels on the large flat screen that hung on the wall. After coming to the conclusion that there was nothing on, I decided to go for a walk and do some shopping in the area. I went in my room and pulled out my Roberto Cavalli jeans and tank top with my Louis Vuitton sneakers. I unwrapped my hair and headed out.

When I got down to the lobby, I took notice to the nice gift shops that I didn't notice before. I started to get a few items but then thought *who the hell am I getting them for?* As I made my way towards the front entrance I had my head down texting Monica so I could tell her I was out shopping, and I could show her the courtesy that she had not been showing me. I was about half way through the text and clearly not paying attention when I bumped into someone.

"I am so sorry," I said, before I looked up and saw Bruno.

"Oh it's all good Tiff. Where you in a rush to?" he asked smiling.

"Hey Bruno. I was bored, so I was gonna do some shopping and grab a bite to eat."

"All by ya' self?"

"Uh. I am a big girl, besides Monica is sleep, and I take it Michelle is out of it too since she didn't answer the door. What you doing back here already?"

"Oh I came to drop Michelle off some bread, but since she sleep that can wait. Why don't we go shopping and get something to eat together, my treat."

"Are you offering to pay for my lunch or my shopping?"

"Both baby, my money is long."

"Well good, because it's gonna be a long afternoon," I joked while being very serious.

Today Bruno drove his midnight blue BMW 745i. It was parked right in front, he tipped the valet as I stood at the passenger side door and waited for him to open it, but that never happened, instead he walked his rude ass around to the driver's side and got in. I rolled my eyes and got in, and before I could put my seatbelt on he pulled off into the Manhattan traffic. My intentions were to have some type of dialogue with him during the car ride, but this nigga stayed on the phone the whole time. He had money, but he was careless. I heard things I'm sure I should not have been

122

hearing. That's how Travon got away with so much, he was very careful about what I heard and what I saw, but this nigga was talking about stash spots, shootings, and everything. Shit, even I knew that was a no no.

In a few minutes we pulled up in front of a restaurant called Masa. It was a very nice looking Japanese spot. Once again, he passed the keys to the valet while still not hanging up the phone. He motioned with his head for me to follow him. He had no manners or couth whatsoever. When we got inside the restaurant I noticed how nice the décor was. We sat at the sushi bar, where the surface of the bar was carved out of a rare Japanese wood, I was told later that the bar itself cost sixty thousand dollars, which would explain why the average meal on the menu was priced between four hundred and six hundred dollars. We had been seated for about five minutes and this nigga was still on the phone. I had enough.

"Um hello. Can you hang the phone up?"

He gave me a look that showed his disapproval of my request, so I shot him a look right back that said I didn't give a fuck.

"Yo man, go ahead and handle that shit and I'm gonna hit you in a few," he said giving in.

"That's more like it," I joked.

"Yo Ma. Don't ever do that shit again. When I'm on the phone you chill the fuck out and don't be so rude. You feel me?" he said calling himself scolding me but I played along.

"My bad boo. I just don't know how much time we have and I wanted your undivided attention," I lied.

"Well we are in no rush so just relax. Order whatever you want."

"What do you suggest?"

"Shit I don't know. I always get the chicken. I keep it simple," he replied being no help at all.

I damn sure was not going to just order chicken. I was going in for the kill. Travon had always taught me to never settle for anything less than the best and that's what I planned on doing. The waiter came and I proved my point.

"Arigato. Can I start you off with a cocktail?" he said with a bow.

I knew waiting for Bruno to be a gentleman and order for me would be pointless so I went in for myself.

"Yes. I'll have the Raspberry Champagne Cocktail" I responded. I never had it before but it sounded good. It was Japanese shiso leaf, fresh raspberry puree, and la caravelle champagne.

"Excellent choice and for you sir?"

"Yeah lemme' get a shot of patron and a corona with lemon," Bruno responded.

"Okay your drinks will be right out. Are you ready to order, or do you need more time?"

"No I'm ready. I'll have the Lobster and Chanterelle Risotto, the Wagyu Beef Tataki with summer truffle and Spicy Dancing Shrimp."

"Another excellent choice, and for you sir?"

"Give me the Hibachi chicken and white rice," Bruno responded with his plain ass.

"Any appetizers?" The waiter continued, Bruno waived him off but I stopped him.

"Yes please. I'll have the seasonal Sashimi tasting."

"Very well," he said as he took the menus and left.

"Damn girl you can eat huh?" Bruno said going in on me.

"Shit. I need something to soak up all this liquor from last night."

"I can dig it. So tell me about you Tiffany?"

"What do you want to know?

"Well. Were you born and raised in Baltimore?"

"Yup. All my life," I lied.

"Okay so how did you meet Michelle?"

Damn. I knew that question was coming up. The problem is I had no idea what Chelle had already told him.

"Damn Bruno. You writing a book or you the police?" I asked dancing around the question.

"Nah. I ain't writing a book, and I damn sure ain't the police. I was just curious. Ya'll seem like night and day. You carry ya 'self on a whole 'nother level. "

"What you mean by that?" I asked already knowing the answer to the question.

"For instance, she would have never ordered the shit you just ordered. She probably can't even pronounce the shit keeping it real. And she dresses nice and all, but your aura is just crazy. I can tell you been around money before."

"Hold up. Don't be trying to play my girl," I said laughing.

"I ain't playing her. I just call it like I see it. It seems like she knows how to spend other niggas money. You on the other hand, seems like you have had your own before."

"Look Bruno, let's just say I ain't green to the shit that goes on in these streets. And I have been around the finest shit in life, so I carry myself as such. My girl Chelle know about money too, don't get t twisted," I said, trying to defend her but knowing that what he said was the truth.

The waiter brought our drinks, bowed and left.

"Let's toast," Bruno said raising his shot glass.

"And what exactly are we toasting to?"

"Our new friendship."

"Oh is that what this is?"

"No doubt. You don't have a problem with that do you?"

"No, but Chelle might."

"Look I take good care of Michelle, and the money that I spend on her buys me certain privileges and freedoms," he said throwing back his shot of Patron and taking a sip of his Corona.

"What kind of privileges and freedoms?" I asked, sipping my drink.

"The no questions asked type," he answered matter of factly.

"I hear that hot shit."

"Yeah well it is what it is. So I'll ask again. Do you have a problem with our new friendship?"

"No baby. Not at all," I replied smiling as our food came.

For the next few hours we ate, drank, and shopped endlessly. Bruno was very rough around the edges, but once you get through his asshole interior, he was actually okay to be around. I could kind of see why Michelle was all dumb over him. When we pulled up to the hotel Michelle was sitting in the courtyard having a drink, her eyes got as big as the Brooklyn Bridge when Bruno called the porter over to help unload and carry all of my bags.

"Hey girl what's good?" I asked.

"Umm where you been?" she responded as she looked passed me at the car.

"Lunch and shopping."

"With Bruno?"

"Yes. And don't start your shit. We already spoke about this."

"Oh. Nah, it's cool. I was just wondering," she responded as Bruno approached the table.

"What's good Ma?" he asked Michelle.

"Nothing. I was sitting here waiting on you. You still gonna give me some money to go shopping right?

"Here" he said as he pulled some money out his pocket without counting it.

Michelle took it and counted it silently.

"Umm Bruno, what am I supposed to do with a hundred and seventy five dollars? I can't even get a pair of jeans with this," she said disgusted.

"My bad. That's all I got left on me. Tiff done drained me dry. I got you on the next go round," he answered nonchalantly.

She rolled her eyes before he continued.

"A'ight well look I gotta be out. I'll holla at ya'll later," he said kissing *me* on the cheek and heading back to his car and pulling off.

"Excuse me Ma'am, but to which room should I take these packages?" the porter asked.

"Oh you can take them to suite 2903. Thank you very much," I said as I handed him a twenty- dollar bill and watched as he struggled with the overloaded baggage cart.

"So you and Bruno official now?" Michelle asked.

"What you mean official? This is strictly business remember?"

"Yeah. That's what I meant. Did he take the bait? I mean it looks like he did to me."

"Well we'll see. It's still too early to tell. The fact that he just blew a couple of grand don't really mean shit. He could have been just showing off, you feel me?"

"I can dig it, but he ain't never went all out for me like that, girl you must have laid ya "G" down tight."

"Well let's hope so. Anyway, have you seen Monica?"

"Yeah she left a few minutes ago. Bitch walked right passed me and didn't even speak. She just got in her car and left."

"Okay well what you wanna do for our last day here?"

"Hmm. Let's go get naked and do some grown up shit."

"Girl bye. Stop playing."

"Okay. Okay. Let's go see a play or something."

"Lion King?"

"Yeah fuck it. Why not."

"Okay let's go change and tear the city up for our last night."

"I'm with that."

The next morning the three of us were downstairs in the atrium, grabbing a bite to eat and waiting on Bruno to bring Michelle some money before we hit the road to head back to Maryland.

"So tell me again why we didn't just grab something to eat on the parkway? I mean like why are we still here? I'm ready to blow this joint and get back to the crib," Monica said anxious to leave.

"We're leaving. I'm just waiting for Bruno to bring me some money that's all," Michelle responded.

"Well damn. We've been sitting here over an hour. What the fuck? Do he print the money his fucking self? And why he ain't just give it to you yesterday? Oh yeah, that's right. He spent it all on your friend," Monica said antagonizing Michelle.

"There you go with your bullshit. I can't wait to get your ass home grouchy Smurf," I said jumping in.

"Whatever," Monica responded rolling her eyes.

Then, as if on cue, Bruno pulled up, blasting the new Jay-Z record. He was so niggerish. He advised the valet not to move the car and made his way over to us.

"What's good ladies?" He asked.

"Hey daddy. What's up?" Michelle responded grinning from ear to ear.

"Hey Bruno," I responded.

"It's about fucking time. Give this broad her bread so we can get ghost," Monica snapped.

"Damn. Hold up grouchy Smurf," Bruno said going right back at her.

129

"Oh shit. I just called her the exact same shit," I laughed.

"She sure did," Michelle concurred, laughing.

"Whatever. Fuck all of ya'll," Monica said not finding it funny.

"Anyway. You got that for me baby so we can get up out of here?" Michelle asked.

"Yeah this weekend went by too fast, unfortunately we gotta head back to Maryland," I said.

"Yeah well, speaking of that. Why don't you stick around a while longer?" Bruno said.

"Oh fuck no! We are getting the fuck out of here," Monica snapped

"Well I ain't mean you," Bruno responded checking her.

"Oh well Monica, I guess yo ass is riding back by ya self," Michelle chuckled taunting her.

"I wasn't talking about you either Chelle," Bruno said bursting her bubble.

"What?" She said shocked.

"I was talking to you Tiffany. I decided that I want you to stick around a while longer, so I can get to know you better."

"Damn. Umm. I don't know what to say," I responded not believing my ears.

"Well bitch. Let me answer for you. Hell no, she ain't staying. Nigga she don't know you. Fuck outta here young," Monica said spazzing.

"Yeah baby. What the fuck?" Michelle jumped in.

Bruno and I both shot her a look that told her to shut the fuck up.

"Damn Tiffany. I thought you was a grown woman that could make her own decisions," Bruno added.

"Hold up. Hold the fuck up. Everybody just chill for a second. Now, I am grown, and I do make my own decisions, but Monica is right. Nigga I don't know you to be staying out here with you," I responded.

"Look I feel you on that, but Michelle and me been friends for a minute now, she knows I'm good people," he said trying to persuade me.

"Yeah nigga, and how that look, you fucking with this broad and now you tryna holler at my girl? What type of broads you think we are? "Monica barked.

"Bruno do me a favor and wait in the car, while I talk to my girls please," I asked.

"No doubt Ma. Handle ya biz," he said as he returned to his car.

"Now listen. Michelle you don't even have a say so in this so you just fall the fuck back. You already know what it is, and Monica you already knew why we came out here. Now if I got this niggas attention, then let me spin him all crazy so I can get him to do what I need him to do," I said pleading my case.

"And what exactly do you need him to do Tiffany? You don't even have a plan," Monica responded.

"Look. All this time I've been thinking too hard. It's actually quite simple. All I have to do is use Bruno against himself."

"What the fuck does that mean?"

"Like I said, it's simple. This fronting ass nigga wanna be the man so bad. All I have to do is convince him that he will never be the man until he gets rid of Travon. Come on Monica, you been around this nigga. You know his dumb ass can be pushed into doing it. All I gotta do is throw that good old Stiletto Diva training on him and it's a wrap. Ain't that what you taught me? Ain't that what the SD's are about; manipulating niggas to make them do what we want?"

"Yeah Tiff, but those rules apply to taking niggas for they money and shit like that. This move can get your wig pushed back."

"Well like I said before, he can't kill me twice. I'm staying and I'm gonna play this shit out till the end. If I get dealt with, then fuck it, I just get dealt with. What do I have to lose? I'm going on twenty-five, fresh out of federal prison, nothing going for myself, no family, and you are the only friend I have. My mind is made up. I'm staying."

"Can I say something?" Michelle asked.

"No!" Me and Monica both said in unison.

I guess Bruno got tired of waiting in the car like a little kid and made his way back over to us.

"So what's it gonna be? I got moves to make?"

"I'm staying," I answered.

"I'm staying too," Monica chimed in.

"With all due respect Monica, I didn't extended the invite to you."

"Yeah well, I ain't leaving my girl out here alone."

"She's a grown ass woman."

"Nigga she don't know you, so I ain't leaving her."

132

"Bitch, you ain't stayin' up here on my dime. You got the game fucked up," Bruno spat back.

"Motherfucker you the one that got the game twisted. I got my own bread; you see that pretty ass brand new Benz over there? Nigga that's my shit, now you call me out my name again and it's gonna be something. Bet that."

"Okay. Okay. Listen. Bruno, Monica's right. I don't know you, so if you really want me to stay, then she's gonna have to stay with me. At least until I get to know you better," I said interjecting.

"C'mon Ma. Ain't nobody gonna cut you up in pieces and shit. You good money, trust me," Bruno replied still trying to convince me.

"Trust is the last word you should use with me. Monica stays, now you can take it or leave it," I stated firmly.

"Fuck it. A'ight Ma. I guess it is what it is. If that's what it's gonna take to get to know you, then so be it. Just keep her hatin' ass away from me."

"Whatever nigga," Monica spat rolling her eyes.

"Um what about me? How the hell am I supposed to get home?" Michelle asked fuming.

"I guess I gotta put you on a plane, but don't worry I'll keep in touch with you," Bruno said patting Michelle on her ass.

"So are we staying here?" I asked.

"Yeah. I'll pay it up for another week. I'm gonna go do that now."

We waited until he entered the building before we spoke.

"Okay Tiff. You got one week to make something happen and we outta here," Monica said.

"That ain't a lot of time, but okay Monica, whatever," I replied.

"Well I guess I better check the fucking plane schedules," Michelle said.

"There's a Delta flight that leaves out every hour on the hour from JFK," Monica said.

"Damn. How you know?" I asked.

While you was locked up, I did this New York shit a few times. And I ain't always drive up here either," Monica responded.

By this time Bruno was making his way back over.

"Okay. Ya'll are all set up in the same suite."

"Awww thanks sweetie," I said smiling flirtatiously.

"No doubt. I'll be back later to take you to get something to eat and some drinks."

"Alright. I'll be waiting.

"C'mon Michelle. There's a plane leaving in an hour and a half. If we hurry we can beat the traffic.

"Yeah okay. I still ain't feeling this shit, but it's whatever," Michelle said grabbing her Gucci travel bag from under the table.

"Cut the bullshit Ma. I'll send for you again in a few weeks. We can still be cool, plus my nigga Mikey been feeling you since day one."

And with that being said, they turned and left. I got what I was asking for, and now it was do or die... literally.

KISS AND TELL

"Baby wake up, wake up. You're doing it again," Sophia said, shaking me out of my sleep.

I jumped out of my sleep sweating bullets yet again. I had been having these nightmares spells since the whole Baltimore situation. This was the third one this week. I had asked Sophia to stay with me at one of the houses I kept on the low. The spells were bad, and I always preferred to be around Sophia when I was going through them because she would always comfort me and make sure I was alright. She said that she used to have to do the same thing to her brother who had bodied few niggas and went to sleep with their souls from time to time. Janelle on the other hand, did nothing but wake me up and tell me to go back to sleep. She had no empathy or sympathy for me whatsoever. She said that I deserved each and every one of those nightmares and the sleepless nights that came along with them. The nightmares usually came in groups of days so when I got the first one a few days ago, I immediately called Sophia and told her to meet me and stay with me a few days, and she happily agreed like she always did.

"Fuck! I hate these fuckin nightmares," I said as I smashed the glass of cold water that Sophia had given me against the wall.

"It's okay baby. I got you," she said as she tenderly wiped my forehead and face with a cold washcloth.

"It seems like they're getting worse and more graphic each time."

"They're just dreams boo, you'll be fine. That shit will wear off, just like my brothers did."

"Well it's been four fuckin' years. When is this shit gonna stop?"

"In time baby, in time," she said as she held me close with the love, care and concern I only wished Janelle would give me at home.

"Baby you don't understand, up until that shit went down in Baltimore, I had never taken a life before. Did I put serious beating on niggas? Yeah, but I never killed anyone. I mean, I ordered hits when it was absolutely necessary, but I never personally pulled the trigger. D-Boy fucked everything up and I hated to kill him, but he forced my hand, and now I have to live with the fact that I killed my best friend. Now L.V. on the other hand, fuck him, I never liked him anyway. As far as I was concerned he put the battery in D-Boys back to set me up, so I got no remorse about ordering Lorenzo to body that nigga. That bitch Tracy is another one, trying to set me up and double cross me, as much as I did for her, her sick mother and her bastard kids; that's how she repays me? She deserved to get her fucking face blown off. But you know what baby? I've told you before and I'll tell you again. The one soul that really haunts

136

me in these nightmares, the one death that I'm truly sorry for is Tiffany's friend Terri. I simply sent D-Boy over there to scare her, maybe rough her up a bit, but this nigga shoots and kills her. What the fuck was I thinking? Terri was all about money; I could have just paid her not to tell Tiffany that she found out who I was and what I did. I was just so afraid to lose Tiffany that I panicked and sent D-Boy's dumb ass to go and scare the shit out of her, I never meant for her to die."

I stopped ranting and venting long enough to notice Sophia eyes starting to well up with tears, but I was used to it. She always cried when I opened up and vented to her about these stories, sometimes we even cried together.

"Come on now Ma with the tears. Are you trying to get mines started up?" I asked half jokingly.

"I'm sorry baby, but every time you tell me this story it just tears me apart. Sometimes I think despite all of your money and success that you should have just stayed in school."

"Yeah tell me about it. I didn't ask for this shit, now it's in my blood. Baltimore was the first time I bodied a nigga, but it wasn't the last. I curse my moms and pops for forcing this shit on me. I didn't ask for this lifestyle."

"Yeah well you got it now. So you gotta handle it baby, and everything that comes with it, both the good and the bad. The shit gets tough baby, but you got this. I got faith in you," she said as she kissed me, then laid me back and made love to me until we both fell asleep.

A HOUSE IS NOT A HOME

The next day I went back home to Janelle and the kids. I had told her that I was going out of town for a few days on business. I knew she didn't believe me, so I wasn't even sure why I even took the time to conjure up stories again anymore.

"Travon this month's bills came up to a little over thirty-one thousand," Janelle informed me.

"Damn. That's almost ten stacks over the normal amount. Where did that come from?" I asked annoyed.

"Travon it came from this new diamond necklace that I treated myself to a few weeks ago. That's a damn shame you didn't even notice. I haven't taken it off since I bought it."

"My bad baby. You know I got a million and one things on my mind."

"Yeah Travon, and I understand that, but my problem is that you don't know where home is on that list of a million and one things."

"C'mon Janelle. Please don't start. Aren't you and the kids well provided for? You got cars, jewels; your closet is overflowing with everything with every top designer there is, the kids go to the best schools, wear the best gear, we live in a house that costs well over a million dollars. What else could you possibly want?"

"A dedicated husband and father Travon. I mean yeah, I'm from the hood just like you, so the money is all good, and I love our lifestyle, but when is enough gonna be enough? Every time you walk out that door, I gotta wonder if you are gonna walk back through the door, or if I'm gonna get that call or knock on the door in the wee hours of the morning. You think the money makes up for all of that? Shit, you keep my wallet full,so if it was all about the money, you would never hear me complaining. The kids and me are gonna get ours regardless. Hell Travon. I even accept the other women that you claim don't exist, but you didn't marry a fool. I know your extra marital activities come with the territory. I'm even still here after that whole Baltimore fiasco stood by your side during the trial and everything. I had my mother lie and forge documents saying that you worked for her company. I lied to our kids about the whole situation. I did all of that while holding your hand and holding my head high like a good wife is supposed to do. So baby what I'm saying is, your wife is a rider, but you gotta give me something besides money to ride for. What is it gonna take for you to leave them streets alone? I guess what I'm trying to say is, despite all my bitching and complaining, I don't wanna lose you, because I wouldn't know what to do without you baby. All the money in the world can't replace you," she said with tears in her eyes.

Damn. Her words were soft, sweet, and sincere. I can't remember the last time she spoke to me like this. In one breath she had managed to make me feel like the best thing since sliced bread, and a piece of shit husband and father all at the same time. And she was a hundred percent right. I needed to get my shit together. It's just that the money came too easy, and too fast for me to just say fuck it and go legit. I mean, the club pulled in money, but not enough to maintain my lifestyle, and call it niggerish, but downsizing was not an option. Now the part about fucking around with different chicks, I had downsized that a long time ago. The only one I dealt with on a serious basis was Sophia and that was something I didn't know if I could ever stop.

"Well Travon, don't just stand there baby. Say something."

I clawed my thoughts for a suitable response, but was saved by the bell when the house phone rang.

"Do not think you are getting out of this conversation Mr. Outlaw," she joked as she answered the phone.

"Hello?"

"*Hey Janelle.*"

"Hey Sophia what's up?"

"*Nothing much. Just trying to track down your big head ass husband. I've been calling his cell for like an hour and I'm getting no answer.*"

"Well he's right here. Is everything okay?"

"*C'mon girl, you know I can't go there with you for legal reasons. Just let me holler at him real quick.*"

"Okay here he goes."

"*Thanks. Let's get together this weekend for drinks. It's been a minute.*"

141

"Okay girl just call me," Janelle said finally handing me the phone.

"Yo what up?" I asked wondering why she didn't call my cell.

"Tray I have been trying to call your cell for almost an hour."

I looked at my cell and confirmed eighteen missed calls and twenty-one text messages.

"Damn, I'm looking at the missed calls now. I must have hit the silent button by accident. What's going on?"

"Well Derrick Anderson is having a party tomorrow and he said Fat Cory is bringing a dish."

"Are you fucking kidding me? Was I invited?"

"Yup. You are his plus one."

"Damn. I guess I better run out and get something to wear."

"Yeah. Why don't you ask him what he's wearing so ya'll don't dress alike? I heard he's over at M&M's getting twisted right now."

"Okay. I'm on my way over there right now."

"Send him my regards."

"You already know," I said as I hung up the phone and turned around to see Janelle shaking her head with her arms folded.

"Look baby. You already know what it's hitting for," I said grabbing my Desert Eagle from the nightstand drawer.

"Have you seen my watch?"

"Which one? You got dozens of them. And speaking of watches, when are you going to throw them three old raggedy ones in your jewelry closet away. Them shits don't even work. They got the wrong time and everything."

"I aint never throwing those away. My pops gave me those. I keep them for sentimental reasons. So please, when you are doing your cleaning and shit. Don't touch them. I want to keep them just the way he left them to me."

"Whatever Travon. Our conversation will resume when you come back."

"Okay boo, I promise," I said kissing her on her forehead and heading out of the bedroom.

"Hey Travon," she replied stopping me in my tracks.

"Make sure you come back to me."

"Always," I said as I jetted out of the house.

I jumped in my 2013 charcoal grey Acura NSX and cursed out loud as I deciphered Sophia's message and replayed it. What she really said was; The D.A. (the initials for Derrick Anderson) was having a meeting (a party) and Fat Cory (this low level street nigga) was bringing a dish (information) and I was his plus one (the info was about me). As my history shows, one thing I will not tolerate is a snitch. What makes it so bad, was this nigga Fat Cory wasn't even on my payroll. He belonged to my home girls Mary and Mekkah. They owned a One Stop Shop in the hood called M&M's. At their spot you could get anything from pussy to heroin and some of the largest poker and dice games were hosted there. On any given night you could walk out winning or losing a hundred grand or more. Mary was a wild bitch from Brooklyn and was always about getting that money. Mekkah was from Philly but got money wherever her big titties and ass would take her, and both of them would go to the guns with any nigga breathing. But they rarely had any problems for two reasons. First off, both of the niggas they fucked with was off the chain. They had both put in some work for me and got themselves jammed up. The Feds put the thumbs to them and they both kept it one hundred and didn't say a fuckin word. We will have four more black presidents before either of them would see the light of day again, but they took their punishment like real stand up G's do. That's why M&M's was the only operation in my district that was able to operate rent free. The second reason is because although everyone knew that their boyfriends would never see the light of day again, Mary and Mekkah were protected by me and everyone who worked for me, which is why I was shocked by Fat Cory's actions, but I would never second guess Sophia's information. For all intents and purposes, she was the horse and I always got it right from her mouth. I called over to M&M's to make sure Fat Cory was still there and to make sure he stayed there.

"M&M's"

"What up Mekkah"

"Who this Travon?"

"You already know."

"Damn nigga. We ain't seen or spoke to you in a minute. When you coming through?"

"I'm actually on my way there right now."

"Word. That' what's up. Wait till I tell Mary. You want me to set you up? I got some new bitches on deck. Bad Cuban bitches flown in from Miami."

"Nah baby. Unfortunately this ain't no social call."

"Oh shit. What's wrong?"

"The roof is leaking over there."

"Get the fuck out of here. Are you serious?"

"Yeah. I'm dead serious."

"Well who fucked the roof up?"

"Fat Cory, and he goin' around saying I did it."

"Say word. That nigga is at the bar right now getting ripped."

"I know. Make sure he don't leave so we can fix the roof when I get there."

"Fuck. This roof ain't never leaked the whole six years we been here, but it is what it is. I'll let the squad know. See you when you get here."

"No doubt."

"A yo Tray."

"What up?"

"I'm sorry."

"Don't be. Ya'll are gonna fix the roof, I'm just gonna supervise. Give me like ten minutes."

"A'ight."

I hung up the phone and drove as fast as I could without getting pulled over. I couldn't risk Fat Cory leaving and making it to that meeting tomorrow. I pulled up in front of M&M's and was pleased to see Fat Cory's Escalade parked on the block. I was sure it was his because of the personalized license plate that simply read FAT CORY. That's probably what got his dumb ass jammed up in the first place. I parked a few cars away and made my way to the front door. I rang the buzzer and looked into the security camera, within seconds I was buzzed in.

Once inside I was greeted promptly by Tree. She was a tall thick chocolate skinned dime that took no shit, and held the door down as if her life depended on it.

"What's up Tray? Long time no see," she said nodding in Fat Cory's direction.

"What's good Ma? I'll be back."

As I approached the end of the bar where Fat Cory was sitting, I watched him struggle to keep his balance as he threw back yet another shot of Patron.

"What up Fat Cory?" I asked as I pat him on the back and sat next to him.

"Oh shit. What's good Tray?" he said, as his eyes got as big as the wheels on his truck he had parked outside.

"Ain't shit. I ain't been here in a minute, so I figured I'd come down and get some relaxation. You feel me?"

"Yeah man. You see I'm down here getting it in. Shit. I'm really trying to go downstairs and get up on some of them hoes, but them bitches is charging an arm and a leg," he said slurring his words.

"I can dig it. That's why I came down here to do. Get a bottle and twist one or two of them bitches out. I heard they just imported a whole squad of Cubans from Miami."

"Word?" I'm trying to see what that's hitting for, but my bread ain't as long as yours."

"Come on son. You know how I do. Come on downstairs and let's blow some money on them hoes. Fuck it. We can't take it with us and any day might be our last. You feel me?"

"Shit nigga. I don't know about you, but I'm gonna live forever," he continued slurring his words with his eyes half closed.

"I feel you fam. That's a great attitude to have. Hey Rhonda, let me get a magnum of Ace Of Spades and put it on my tab," I yelled to one of the bartenders.

"Here you go baby," she said handing me the large bottle and two glasses."

"Thanks sexy. Come on fam," I said helping Fat Cory down off of his stool.

We made our way through the trap house, being acknowledged by people giving me head nods as they watched me lead the proverbial lamb to slaughter. When we got to the door that lead to the basement action, Big Steve the mammoth sized human being that guarded the door stepped in front of it.

"Hold up fellas, you know the rules," he said as he proceeded to pat Fat Cory down.

"You can get this back when you come back upstairs," he said removing a 9mm from Fat Cory's waistband. Then he proceeded to pat me down. He ran his hand right over my big ass Desert Eagle, but left it alone because he knew better.

"Okay fellas enjoy, and don't forget to be gracious with when you tip the ladies," he said opening the door and allowing us entrance.

"Yo Travon, I owe you big time my G. I'm about to tear one of these bitches out the frames," Fat Cory said sounding just as thirsty as he really was.

"Yeah well make sure you enjoy yourself."

When we got downstairs, girls were on stage dancing; there were a few niggas there who left when we walked in. Mary and Mekkah came over to greet us.

"Traaay. Long time no see baby," Mary said hugging me and kissing me on my cheek.

"Hey Ma. What's good?" I responded.

"What's up Fat Cory?" Mekkah asked.

"Hey boss lady," he replied.

"Ya'll come on in and relax," Mary said as her and Mekkah led us into the private room that was illuminated with a black light.

"You guys need anything?" Mekkah asked.

"Yeah. Send in them new Cuban broads and oh yeah, send Kyia too. Have them bring some condoms, more glasses, and make sure we ain't disturbed. I'm gonna make sure my nigga Fat Cory has a good time tonight."

"Okay Boo. I got you. Coming right up," Mekkah replied as they left.

In what seemed like only seconds, in walked two beautiful Cuban chicks and Kyia. Kyia was thicker than your average dancer/escort, but she was pretty as fuck with some of the biggest titties I had ever seen. We actually nicknamed her Nips, due to her fifty-cent sized areolas. Don't get it fucked up, although Kyia was thick as fuck, she was thorough and she made that money. Make no mistake about it, once she threw that good shit on you, you was coming out ya pockets. She also had a twin sister I didn't mind knocking off.

I popped the top on the bottle and poured some for all of us. Kyia reached in her bra and pulled out a baggy of coke.

"Powdered sugar anybody?" she asked showing off what she had.

"Let me get that," Fat Cory said with his mouth watering.

"Uh uh daddy, that ain't no fun. Do it like this," she instructed as she took both breasts out of her bra and sprinkled large amounts of coke on each.

"That's what the fuck I'm talkin' about," Fat Cory responded snorting both piles up like a vacuum.

"Mmm. That turns me on. Now let me return the favor," Kyia said as pushed him back on the red leather couch and unzipped his pants.

She pulled out his dick and was just about to sprinkle some coke on it, but she stopped.

"No baby. This will never work," she said holding his limp dick in her hand as she took it in her mouth while me and the Cuban broads watched.

"Yo Tray, why you ain't getting up on dem pretty bitches fam'? Stop watching me. When I'm done with Kyia, I want one of them bitches."

"Yeah, he's right Papi. Lay back, relax and let us take care of you," one of the Cubans said, attempting to push me back onto another couch.

"Hold up Ma. I'm good for now. Let me get my mind right with this drink, and I'll be more than ready for ya'll, but for now, ya'll go over there and help Nips take care of my man," I instructed as I sat down and filled my glass.

149

The Cubans did as they were told and moved to the next couch and began to strip Fat Cory naked.

"Son you missing out like a motherfucker," he said overly excited.

"Trust me. I'm gonna grab one up as soon as I get my mind right," I said holding my glass up.

I watched as they each took turns sucking and seducing Fat Cory. He was so drunk and high that he was just rambling on and on about nothing. He was saying everything from telling Kyia that he was in love with her, to asking the Cubans if they were related to Fidel Castro. The coke must have been taking effect because even as Kyia rode him like a champ, he just kept talking a mile a minute.

"Damn Kyia, niggas was right. You got that wet wet for real girl. That's my word I would make you my main jump off bitch and ya'll Cuban hoes is bad as fuck too. I think we should all take a vacation or a cruise or something and just fuck all crazy. We can go wherever ya'll wanna go. I mean I ain't got money like that nigga over there, but I got a little somethin' somethin' ya mean?" he rambled.

"You know what your problem is Cory? You talk too fuckin much," Kyia responded not breaking her stride.

"Okay, okay baby. I'll be quiet, just don't stop," he pleaded.

"No nigga. I mean you literally talk too fuckin' much," Kyia replied as she pulled a straight razor from her bra.

Fat Cory's eyes got big as a house, as Kyia began slashing him viciously, sending blood splattering everywhere. The Cubans followed suit and spit razors from their mouths, as the onslaught of razors cut through his flesh like loose leaf paper. I got up and moved out of the way as some of the blood splatter got on my Gucci jacket. Fat Cory screamed in anguish as he tried with all of his might to fight off the octopus-like attack.

"You fucking bitches. I'm gonna fuckin' kill you. You too Travon. You are a dead man you hear me motherfucker?" he said spitting blood from his mouth. He fought to try and get up, but the drugs, alcohol, and rapid blood loss rendered him powerless.

"Guess you gonna be late for your meeting with the District Attorney's office you faggot motherfucker," I hissed.

"Go to hell Travon," he spat.

"Maybe, but since you will be there first save me a spot. Continue ladies," I instructed as I calmly sipped my drink.

"Yo hold this bitch ass nigga down," Kyia demanded as the Cubans did what they were told.

Fat Cory fought and squirmed, but his efforts were fruitless as Kyia straddled him, forced her hand into his mouth, grabbed his tongue and cut it out. Fat Cory wailed like a banshee holding his mouth as if he could stop the bleeding that way. We all stood back and watched as he writhed in pain. A few second later Mekkah walked in carrying a chrome .380. Without saying a word, she walked up to Fat Cory and put a bullet right through his left eye, sending blood and brain fragments splattering against the wall behind him, killing him instantly.

"Damn that was come cold blooded shit," I said.

"Yeah, well I was watching from the video monitor in my office and ya'll was taking too long with this motherfucker," Mekkah responded.

"I just wanted him to suffer a little bit, but Kyia and the Cuban connection over there looked like they were having so much fun that I just let them rock out," I joked.

"Well with all due respect, I got a business to run and for every minute ya'll got this room closed I'm losing thousands of dollars. Ya'll ladies get this room cleaned up so I can get back to this money, I'll have Big Steve get rid of the body," Mekkah instructed.

"Well the newbies are gonna have to handle that. I'm about to take a shower and be out," Kyia responded.

"What? Where you going Kyia? Mekkah asked.

"Girl it's Saturday and it's late. You know I got church in the morning.

"OMG bitch. Call me tomorrow. Ya'll hoes go to the supply closet get some bleach, lye, a bucket of water, some scrub brushes and get to work. You got one hour. I want this shit spotless," Mekkah barked.

"A'ight. Well I'm about to get up out of here. I'll holler at ya'll later. It might be time for ya'll to do some spring cleaning around here so shit like this don't happen again," I said pouring the remainder of my bottle out on Fat Cory's lifeless body.

"Yeah Travon. About that, here, me and Mary want you to have this," she said handing me an envelope.

"What's this?"

"Twenty five thousand. Let's call it an inconvenience fee."

"Nah. I'm cool. What I look like taxing ya'll?"

"Travon we fucked up. We had a fucking snitch in our house and that shit almost got you jammed up. Now if it was anybody else, you would have taxed them or did something worse for the fuck up. We want to be held to the same standards."

"Okay I'll take it," I said accepting the envelope.

"Good."

"Now I'm donating it to you and Mary's kids college fund. Look, I gotta go," I said handing her the envelope back and hugging her.

"Damn you Travon. Call me tomorrow."

"Okay, and have somebody get Fat Cory's truck from around here."

"No doubt, I'm on it," she replied as I made my way out the back door.

I hoped I could make it back into the house without Janelle seeing this blood on my jacket.

SLEEPING WITH THE ENEMY

"You know we gonna have to deal with this nigga now right? Fuck!" Bruno yelled, as he hung up his cell phone.

"What's wrong baby? I asked as I lay across his chest.

"Nothing Ma. Just business that's all."

"Well it sounds serious, so tell me what it is."

"Look Tiffany. I don't be discussing my business with just anybody. Okay?"

"Oh now I'm just anybody? Last night you were telling me how special and different I was. You also said you wanted me to stay out here and be your rider; you further went on to say how much you was feeling me. Oh let me guess, you were saying that to get the pussy huh? Well let me put you on nigga. I was gonna give you the pussy anyway because I was feeling your style, but after that lame ass move, I'm ready to get back to Maryland. I can't believe you tried to play me like I was one of those green ass broads you're used to fucking with. Where's my cell? Let me call

Monica and tell her this trip is over," I said attempting to win an Oscar, and bait him in, as I paced back and forth butt ass naked pretending to look for my cell phone.

"Hold on Tiff. I did mean all of that shit, but there are certain things about me that you don't need to know. Trust me; it's for your own good. I'm really feeling you Ma, and although it's plain to see what I do for a living, if we gonna fuck with each other then I wanna keep you sheltered from that part of my life," he responded damn near begging.

"Look Bruno. My ex called himself sheltering me too. He kept things from me, very important things. So when shit hit the fan, and them Feds kicked my door in, there wasn't shit I could do but watch them take his ass away. All his so called boys that he trusted split up all his work and all of his money that he had in the streets. They didn't leave any money for his mother, his kids, or me. It's a good thing that when they came for his stash, I kept a nice chunk of it just in case they tried some bullshit; which they did," I said, lying my ass off, but loving the story.

"Say word Ma. That's what's up. So what you do with the work you pinched?" he asked now fully engulfed in the story.

"Well, I was forced to become a drug dealer overnight. I called my home girl, because I knew her man was in the streets doing his thing and I knew he wouldn't try to get over on me, so I sold him everything at a discounted rate," I continued, not believing how well the story was rolling off my tongue.

"Damn. How much shit was it?"

"Let's just say it was enough for me to get by on for a few years."

"So what did you do with the money?"

"I held him down and took care of his books, dropped money off to his kids' moms every month, and took care of his mother, like a real rider and wifey was supposed to do."

"What do you mean like a wifey *was* supposed to do?"

"I mean I held him down faithfully for six years until he was killed in prison."

"Damn, that's crazy. I'm sorry to hear that."

"Don't be. It's part of the game. The moral of the story is, by keeping me out of the loop I couldn't be that rider that he needed. He put his trust in his boys and it cost him his money, and ultimately his life. Ya'll niggas kill me. Don't ya'll know that back in the day every successful Emperor and King consulted the Queen before they made any decisions? The great kingdoms were ruled together. The Kings that tried to have the Queen play the background; they all fell on the enemy's sword."

"Damn, I had a feeling you was a little more thorough than the average, but I had no idea you was on point like that. I could use somebody like that in my corner. I might have to keep you around longer than we talked about."

He had taken the bait.

"Nah I gotta get back in a few days."

"What's your rush? What do you have to go back to? Do you got kids?"

That question almost made me cry instantly.

157

"Nope. No kids."

"Well if it's your job that you're worried about, I will double whatever your paycheck would normally be."

"Nigga do I look like a nine to five bitch to you?"

"Not at all."

"Alright then."

"So what are you rushing back to?"

"A life where I'm comfortable and well taken care of."

"And you don't think I can do that for you?"

"I'm sure you could, but I ain't with all of this secretive shit you on. I ain't trying to be left in the dark and out in the cold ever again."

"Nah it ain't even like that. Listen, you fucked my head up with the history lesson about the Emperors and shit, and then when you told me your own story, I was hooked."

"Hmm. Well I did always want to move to New York."

"Say no more. I got an extra apartment fully furnished. You can have it."

Damn. His last statement sent chills through my body. Not because they turned me on, but because it was almost that exact same sentence that got me fucked up with Travon's trifling ass. I was suddenly getting cold feet, as his offer brought back four years of nightmares.

"Hello. Earth to Tiffany," he called snapping me out of my daydream.

"Huh?" I said sounding lost.

"Well what's it gonna be? You riding with me or not?"

158

"I'm not sure yet. Let's see how these next few days go."

"Fair enough, but I'm sure I can convince you."

"We shall see, but for now come back over here and give me some of that good New York loving."

"Say no more," he said as he climbed back into bed.

A few hours later I woke up to the sound of Bruno snoring. While he may have thought he threw the dick on me all crazy, he had no idea that I was faking every bit of it. He, on the other hand, was sleeping like a baby. One thing I didn't forget while I was locked up was how to throw this cat on a nigga and put him to bed. Although it did feel weird because Travon was the only man I had ever slept with before.

I looked over at Bruno and he was curled up like a newborn baby in the fetal position, snoring away. All he was missing was his thumb in his mouth. I was just now getting a good look at his apartment, because by the time we got here last night I just wanted to go to bed, but of course he just wanted to fuck. In any event, I never got to check out the place. For all the money he had, Bruno was your typical small-minded drug dealer. The apartment was a moderate sized two bedroom, one bathroom; of course there was a large plasma TV that hung from the wall in the living room. There was an X-Box 360 connected to it and there were games scattered all over the floor. His living room furniture was a dated money green leather sofa and love seat. The carpet was beige and looked like it had not been steam cleaned in God knows how long. His bedroom had a queen-sized bed with a black leather padded headboard. On the dresser was a mirror that had pictures of him and his boys at the club wedged into the creases and an assortment of chains and diamond medallions hanging from the corners. Diamond bracelets and watches just laid across the dresser, no jewelry box or nothing. The place looked so bland and plain, that I thought it might be a trap house, but there were no extra locks on the door and even Bruno wasn't that stupid, so I concluded that this must be his crib. There was what seemed to be a couple thousand dollars sprawled across the dresser and a few stack on the nightstand along with his pistol. This guy was a real piece of work. What was to stop me from robbing him blind while he slept? Instead, I decided to wake him, I had done enough acting for the day. I was ready to go back to the hotel so I could wash his wackiness off of me. He was definitely no Travon.

On the way back to the hotel, Bruno was once again yelling and cursing on his cell phone. Something was wrong and I wanted to know what it was, especially if it involved Travon. I waited until he hung up and sprung the interrogation on him.

"Okay now, all day you've been on the phone, and all day you've been cursing somebody out. Now what's wrong Bruno?"

"Come on Ma. I thought we talked about this already."

"You're right and obviously you didn't hear a word I said. Just forget it Bruno. Don't worry about it. I'm good."

Bruno stayed silent for a minute and then put his foot right in my bear trap.

"So you tryna' be my Queen and rule with me side by side huh?"

"I was considering it, but you play way too many games. I told you I'm not going into anything blind ever again. "

"Okay. I'm gonna put you on Tiffany, but you better not cross me, or that's word to my man Black may he rest in peace, it's gonna be a problem."

"Oh now you threatening me? Never mind Bruno. Fuck it. We can just be cool and chill from time to time. I'm cool," I said resetting the trap.

"Nah baby, I ain't threatening you. I'm just saying, I'm not used to sharing certain things with people, but you're right. Things are a little fucked up right now, so maybe I do have tunnel vision and need a fresh set of eyes and ears on the situation."

"That's what I'm here for baby. That's what Queens do, they hold their Kings down."

"Oh are we King and Queen now?"

"That is entirely up to you. Now give me the run down."

"Well the problem is, somebody I got working for me disappeared with four bricks of that white."

"Yeah I can see how that could be a small problem, but you'll get the work back. I'm more concerned with the dude that ran off with it."

"Oh don't worry about him, once my wolves track him down, he gonna have a bad fucking day. It's them four bricks that I'm worry about."

"Babe, the bricks should be the least of your concerns. You should be more concerned with the fact that the guy who stole the shit obviously had no respect for you. You can have all the money in the world, but if you don't have respect in this game, you don't have shit. Now I ain't no guru on this drug shit, but I know four bricks is a lot, and once word gets out that you got burned for such a large amount, it's going to be open season on you."

"Tiffany I'm trying to tell you, I can't be worried about that right now. I'm gonna have to answer for them bricks, and it ain't gonna be pretty."

"Come on baby. Who do *you* have to answer to? You run this shit don't you?" I asked hoping I pushed the right button that would open him right up.

"Baby, everybody has a boss and the dude I pick my work up from ain't gonna be too pleased with the fact that I'm in the hole for four bricks. That's over a hundred grand. Shit. We had a falling out over only three thousand before," he said sounding more worried that he probably wanted to.

"Okay don't get all flustered, this can be worked out. From what I can see you make a lot of money for yourself, so that tells me that you make a hell of a lot more for this dude that you pick up from. So it's common sense that he won't want to lose your portion of his income. So maybe you and this dude can work out some sort of payment plan. By the way, I'm tired of saying *this dude,* what's his name?"

Listen Tiffany; this shit ain't like a big ass cable bill. I can't just put a little something on it. This nigga is gonna want all of his money up front."

"Okay Bruno, so give it to him; and what is his name?"

"I ain't got no hundred racks to be just giving away, and his name is Travon damn. Does knowing his name lower the cost of the debt or something?"

"Don't snap out on me. I didn't get you into this mess, but I'm trying to help you figure a way out of it. Now in the few days that I've been here, I've seen you drive over two hundred thousand dollars worth of cars including this one, not to mention all of the jewelry, which is probably another hundred grand or more. So why in the hell don't you have a hundred stacks to pay this Travon guy?"

"Look Ma. The money comes in, and it goes back out. Nobody keeps track of that shit. You ball out, till you fall out. That's what this life's about, period, point blank."

Stupid ignorant ass niggas. I thought to myself.

"Okay soooo you never thought to put anything away for a rainy day, savings, or just such an occasion? I asked perplexed.

"First off, I didn't say I didn't have the money. I said I didn't have it just to hand over to that nigga. I ain't gonna lie, that shit would cut kind of deep," he replied finally keeping it real.

I saw my window of opportunity and jumped through.

"Okay babe, then in that case, it's simple, fuck Travon. Don't pay him. Take whatever you got in the stash and cop from somebody else. He ain't the only candy store in town, I'm sure."

"That will never work. That would start a crazy ass war with him and his people, and you're wrong, Travon runs this city, everything goes through him. So even if I did cop from somebody else, it would have to be somebody from out of town, and even then I wouldn't be able to move it without a problem from Travon."

"Well Bruno, let me ask you a question. If you were in a rush to get somewhere right now and your life depended on getting there, you had no time to stop or make detours, and something was in the middle of the road; what would you do?"

"If my life depended on it, I'd run that motherfucker over."

"Well that's what you have to do with Travon, same principles apply."

"Body Travon? You think it's that easy huh?"

"You said you was gonna get rid of the dude who stole from you. I'm just saying; if you can have him taken care of, then you can have this Travon guy taken care of. In my opinion, you are way too smart to be working for anybody but yourself. Shit, in just these few days I could sense how powerful you are. A little rough around the edges, but powerful."

"Hold up. What you mean rough around the edges?" he asked sounding a little offended.

"I mean for somebody who gets money like you baby, you are all over the place. Your apartment is a mess, you dress like a typical hood nigga when we go out, you order typical hood shit to eat, and you carry yourself in a typical hood manner. I mean come on, who has over two hundred thousand dollars worth of cars and jewelry and lives in an apartment? Your priorities are all fucked up. If you think small, you will be small. I bet Travon got his shit all the way together, and if you gonna get on his level, do it one hundred percent. Don't worry, I'm gonna whip you into shape," I said joking, but dead serious.

"Oh is that right?"

"Yeah. That's what I do. I hold true kings down," I said caressing his free hand.

"Okay Ma, we'll see," he responded showing a slight smile.

STAYING PUT

"Wake up hoe," Monica said jumping on my bed like a big kid.

"Come on bitch stop. I'm trying to sleep," I replied tired and irritated.

"Get ya ass up. You been out every night with that lame ass nigga Bruno and I want details, but more importantly I want to know when we getting the fuck back to the crib? I'm down to my last three thousand and I done maxed out three credit cards, fucking with you and this wack ass extended stay."

"Get your thick ass up of me. It ain't nothing to tell," I responded pushing her off me and sitting up.

"Okay so we've been here all this time for you to get dick and gifts? Bitch I could have got you more gifts, with less dick, in half the time back home."

"Whatever. Your ass been creeping with this mystery nigga, just as much as I have been with Bruno, so shut the hell up," I joked.

"Well if your master plan ain't coming together, can we get the hell out of here now?"

"Don't kill me girl, but I need just a little more time to work this nigga. I got him right where on the fence, I just gotta build up enough momentum to push him over."

"No. We had a deal. We got two days left and we are hitting 95 south back to the crib."

"Yeah. I figured you would say that, so I've decided to stay and ride this thing out. If you want to leave then go ahead. I'm close to making something happen. I can feel it in my soul. My mind is made up. There is no turning back for me," I said meaning every word of it.

"I'm not having this conversation with you. I got some runs to make. You need to get your motherfucking mind right and have it right when I get back and maybe we can catch a movie or something."

"We can catch a movie, but there ain't nothing else to think about."

"I'm outta here," she said rolling her eyes and heading out of my room.

"There you go sneaking off again. Why don't you ever take me to meet this mystery nigga?"

"Hmm. Maybe I will. I'm sure you wouldn't want a stranger accompanying me to your fucking funeral," She said sarcastically as she left and slammed the door.

I knew she was pissed, but this was one time in my life that I needed to stick to my guns. Was I playing a deadly game? Most definitely, but what did I have to lose? If shit got funky and I did catch a bad one, at least I would be with my mother and father again. So at the end of the day, this is a win-win situation for me. I didn't expect Monica to understand, but at this point I didn't care.

FIRST BLOOD

I had gotten the call that Bruno and the Baisley crew was done with the four bricks I had given them last week. They said they were done with the four and wanted six more. My instructions from Travon were that as long as the money was straight for the four, I could go ahead and front them six this time instead of the usual four. So I loaded the coke into my trunk, my gun in my purse and headed for Baisley.

When I pulled up in front of Baisley at our normal meeting spot, Bruno's boy Mikey wasn't there. They knew I didn't play that late for the drop shit. I called Bruno to see what the holdup was.

"*Yo*" he said, as he answered the phone

"Where the fuck is your man at Bruno?" I barked.

"*Chill Shanise. He'll be there in a minute. We just wanted to double-check the money. We don't wanna hear ya boy Travon's mouth. So just sit tight. You at the spot?*"

"Yeah nigga. Where else would I be? *I'm* on fucking time."

"*Okay. Calm the fuck down. Which one of your whips you in.?*"

"Motherfucker I'm in the one that's parked at the spot, now hurry the fuck up," I screamed as I hit the end button on my cell.

I sat there for a few more minutes, and then I noticed a black Dodge Challenger pull up behind me. The car wasn't Mikey's and from what I could tell from my rear view, the driver wasn't him either and neither was the nigga in the passenger seat. The driver got out and started heading my way. I eased my pistol out of my purse, cocked it back and placed it on my lap right before he tapped on my window.

"Yeah?" I said as I cracked the window.

"Sorry to bother you pretty, but you're in my parking spot," he said not taking his eyes off of my cleavage.

Red flags immediately went up. I was parked in front of a fire hydrant, so I knew this could not be his parking spot. My survival skills kicked in right away. I rolled my window all the way down.

"I'm sorry daddy, my shit broke down and my cell phone is dead. You mind if I use yours to call a tow truck?"

Before he could respond, I reached out the window and removed the cell phone off his hip.

"Yo shorty what you doing?" he asked caught off guard.

"Oh this will only take a second baby," I answered, as I batted my eyes at him flirtatiously.

My intentions were to scroll through the phone and gather info on this dude as quickly as possible, but before I could start my investigation, an incoming text message flashed across the screen. It was from Bruno and it read:

"What's taking so long? Pop the bitch, snatch the car and get out of there?"

I tried not to show any emotion, as it was now evident that I needed to go on the offensive.

"Baby, can you unlock your phone for me?" I said as I pretended to hand it to him, but purposely dropped it out of the window.

"Come on shorty. What the fuck is wrong with you?" he replied bending down to pick it up.

Once he kneeled down, I swiftly sent two shots through my driver's side door, both shots catching him in the face and spilling what little brains this stupid motherfucker had onto the sidewalk. I put my BMW 645i in drive and stomped on the gas pedal, but not before I heard a barrage of return fire and what sounded like a thousand rocks hitting my car.

The passenger of the Challenger slid over and gave chase. He stuck one hand out of the window and sent several shots in my direction attempting to finish the job that his partner failed at. I tried to successfully navigate my BMW while simultaneously turning around and returning fire through my rear windshield. We continued the high-speed chase, as I cut corners attempting to lose this motherfucker, but he wasn't giving up. Then an idea hit me. At the next corner I hung a left and gunned it with the Challenger still in pursuit. I remembered that today was Baisley Day, which was a day that the projects put together a block party. There would hundreds of kids walking around and if this nigga behind me was from Baisley, chances were that he had a kid or loved one outside and he wouldn't risk hurting them accidentally. Me on the other hand, I didn't give a fuck. I headed straight for the large crowd and just as I expected, the car pulled over and stopped chasing me. I slowed down, made my way through the crowd and headed for the highway. Travon was not going to like this shit one bit.

BEST KEPT SECRET

"You know baby, I can't wait until all of this is over with. All of this sneaking around is killing me."

"Come on Monica. How many times we gotta go through this? We have a plan in motion and as long as you keep Tiffany out of my way, we'll be fine."

"Yeah well, babysitting her is not easy. I can't manipulate her like I did years ago and lying to her in her face every day is getting harder and harder."

"Look. We had a deal. I arrange to get her out of jail and you keep her the fuck away from me. Now you knew keeping her out of my way was going to be a task, but you agreed to it anyway. You still that money hungry broad waiting for the pot of gold at the end of the rainbow that you know I am going to deliver. Now I'm telling you, if you can't keep her out of my way; I promise you she will get hurt."

"Okay baby, Okay. I'll try harder, but she is hell bent on staying out here in New York a little while longer."

"What the fuck is she sticking around for?"

"Baby I don't know. She says she like it and she don't have a reason to rush back."

"Well you better give her a fucking reason."

"Okay. I got you."

MAN OF WAR

"What? Are you okay?" I asked, screaming into my cell phone.

"*Yeah I'm good. Just a little shaken up, and my whip looks like I drove it through Beirut, but other than that I'm fine,*" Shanise answered.

"I can't believe Bruno's bitch ass would even try something like that."

"*Yeah well believe it. That nigga tried to take me out the game and catch you for six bricks, not to mention the four I'm sure he burned us for.*"

"I am going to kill that motherfucker over and over again. Now that I know I ain't got no bread coming out of Baisley, I ain't got shit to lose," I explained pacing back and forth.

"*He had to know this was gonna start a war, but even so, now he is short one soldier.*"

"Oh yeah. You said you caught one of them right?"

"*Fuck yeah. Laid his bitch ass out right in front of the projects.*"

"Good girl. That's what's up."

"*Well I learned from the best baby.*"

"No doubt. Let's squad up and meet at the office."

175

"Okay Tray."

"Hey Shanise. Are you sure you're okay?"

"You got my back Travon?"

"You already know."

"Then in that case, I'm just fine baby," she stated as she hung up the phone.

I called Lorenzo, and filled him in on what had happened. He was on fire.

"Oh my God Tray. Please let me go air them niggas out," he pleaded.

"Come on son. You already know how I do. I play chess, not checkers. Call Jo-Jo and Sayeed and have them meet us at the club."

"Okay. I'm on it."

"Cool. I'm on my way there now."

When I got to the club, Sayeed was already there. Jo-Jo and Lorenzo came soon after me. Shanise was understandably running late. I told her that she didn't have to come, but she was a true rider, and she insisted. I also had Sophia there, but she was there as my legal counsel and not my side chick. I took my customary triple shot of Henny and started the meeting.

"Okay so as I'm sure you heard, shit got real today. I mean shit got really real. For some reason, that nigga Bruno suddenly decided to test me. Now I don't know where he got the heart or the balls from, but at this point it don't matter because I'm gonna rip them shits out." I said pacing back and forth.

"It seems like a simple fix. Just blow that niggas face off, no questions asked," Lorenzo replied.

"It's not gonna be that simple. I'm pretty sure he's gonna get low after the shit he pulled today. Shit. Beat me out of my money, try and rob me for more, and try to hurt somebody close to me? You better get fucking low early," I said fuming.

"Well fuck it then, we'll just go down there every day and tear the projects up. Either we'll flush him out, or the hood will give him up after about the fourth funeral." Jo-Jo added.

"If I may Travon, I understand your frustration Jo Jo, but that is a very bad idea. First off, all you're going to do is make Bruno go deeper into hiding and second, that will bring so much heat down from the police that not only will that force us to stop pursing Bruno, but it may put a dent in the other operations as well." Sophia interjected.

"I agree. We have to be strategic about this. Now it stands to reason that Bruno must be low on cash because if he had his own bread, he wouldn't have tried to steal six bricks from me. He would have just back doored me and copped from the competition."

"Well what's the word on the four bricks from his last order?" Lorenzo asked.

"I'm obviously burned for those, so no sense even adding them to the months count."

There was a knock at the door and I could see from the video monitor that it was Shanise. I walked over to the door and let her in. I couldn't buzz her because I had the door triple locked since Sayeed was in here with me.

"What's good baby? How you feeling?" I asked giving her a hug and a kiss on the cheek.

"I'm good. Like I said earlier, I'm a little shaken up, but I'm more pissed off than anything. My motherfucking car looks like it was used for target practice," she said fuming.

"Ain't that a bitch? Somebody tried to earth you, and all you can think about is that damn car." Sayeed joked.

"Shut up Sayeed. You know the 645 was my favorite whip."

"I know Ma. I'm just fucking with you. I'm glad you're okay."

"Yeah, by the grace of God I'm fine, now what's the plan to get back at these niggas?"

"We were just discussing that when you came in. while I agree with Sophia that we shouldn't just go in the projects with guns blazing, I do believe we need to send a message. So Jo Jo, I want you to send a scout out there over the next few days. I wanna see if they switch up their day-to-day operations and if you see anybody that's directly associated with Bruno I want you to send they mama a black dress. You feel me?"

"No doubt, I'll put some eyes on the block that they ain't never seen before," Jo Jo obliged.

"Sayeed I want you to beef up security here at the club. If he's stupid enough to go after Shanise, he might just be stupid enough to try something here. I can tell this shit is gonna ugly."

"Well what do you want me to do?" Shanise asked.

"I want your little hot headed ass to chill. Knowing you, you'll go on a rampage all by yourself with no back up or nothing," I joked.

"You already know, but I ain't trying to sit around and let ya'll fight my battles," she responded adamantly.

"This ain't just your battle. When he fucked with you, it became our battle and collectively we gonna handle this shit. I don't want anybody caught slipping or taking anything lightly. If you see anything out of the ordinary, ya'll handle that shit accordingly."

"So you giving us the green light?" Sayeed asked.

"I'm saying *if* you come across a situation where shit looks suspect, then yes; shoot first and ask questions last," I confirmed.

"Say no more." Lorenzo chimed in.

"Okay ya'll get back out there to that money and like I said be extra careful. Shanise since Baisley is off the map right now, you hold down Hollis. Jo Jo, you fall back from Hollis and let Shanise get that for now," I instructed.

"With all due respect Tray, that's how I eat my dude," Jo Jo responded.

"Yeah I feel you, but with everything that's going on right now, I need more of your muscle and less of your hustle. Shanise, give Jo Jo twelve percent of the weekly pick up."

"No problem." Shanise concurred.

" Jo Jo I know twelve percent ain't shit compared to what you were originally getting, but you'll also pick up an envelope from me every week to help smooth things over until shit gets back to normal."

"Okay Tray, good looking."

"No doubt. You know I take care of my own. Now we've taken up enough time, let's get back to this money," I said as they dispersed.

PUPPET MASTER

I was awakened with a bucket of ice cold water, followed by slaps and punches to the face.

"Bitch you tryna' set me the fuck up? That nigga Travon sent you here to get at me? Did you think I wasn't gonna find out who you was you dirty bitch?" Bruno said delivering punches to my face and body a million swings a minute.

"Bruno please stop. I don't know what you're talking about," I lied trying to save my life.

"Get the fuck over here you lying bitch. You done fucked with the wrong nigga and you gonna learn today," he screamed, as he grabbed me by my leg, stopping my attempt to scurry away.

When he got me to the edge of the bed, I caught a glimpse of my battered and bloody face in the mirror behind him. I opened my mouth to scream, but he had both hands around my throat attempting to squeeze the life out of me. I felt myself passing out from the lack of oxygen, but he slapped me viciously across the face.

"Nah bitch. You ain't getting off that easy," he taunted as he shoved his gun in my mouth, shattering most of my teeth.

181

"Today is the day you learn that crossing me was a mistake you can never make up for."

My eyes widened as I watched his thumb pull back the hammer on the gun. I then closed my eyes and said a prayer. I had played a dangerous game and lost. I could hear him laughing as he pulled the trigger.

I jumped up from my sleep, drenched in sweat and my heart was pounding through my chest. The nightmare was so realistic that I jumped up out of the bed and rushed to the mirror to inspect my face for damages. To my relief there was no damage, but there were tears streaming down my face. Shit, I must have been crying in my sleep. I washed my face with cold water, took a deep breath and gathered myself. I decided to snatch Monica up for a movie date. I went to her room and knocked.

"Come in."

"Hey girl what's up?" I said plopping down on her bed.

"Nothing much. Just sitting here contemplating what to do."

"What you mean?"

"I mean, I'm ready to get the hell out of here, but I don't want to leave you by yourself."

"Monica I'm grown. I'm so tired of hearing this shit. If you want to leave, just leave. I'll be fine."

"Why the fuck you snapping out?"

"It seems like we have this conversation every day and the shit is getting really old and redundant. You already know I ain't going nowhere, so this shit should be a dead issue."

"You know what? You're right, you grown and you don't need no babysitter. Anyway what's up?"

"Nothing bitch. I was just trying to see if you wanted to go to the movies tonight, but you done pissed me off."

"Oh shut the hell up. What you wanna go see?" she asked.

"Let's go see A Gangster's Melody. I hear they made it into a movie.

"What you mean they made it into a movie? What was it before?"

"Girl that shit was one of the hottest books out. You know I be on them books by the dude Sean A. Wright."

"Oh well you the book worm. I don't know nothing about that shit, but if you wanna go, we can go."

"Okay bet. I'm gonna go get dressed, you get your lazy ass up and do the same."

A few hours later we were in the movie theater enjoying the movie and my cell phone started vibrating. I was going to ignore it, but I saw it was Bruno.

"Hello?" I whispered into the phone.

"*Yo, I been calling you all day. Where are you? And why are you whispering?*"

"I'm at the movies with Monica."

"*Which one?*"

"The one on 34th street"

"*I'm at the hotel. I'm coming to get you. Be outside in ten minutes.*"

"Babe, I'm in the middle of the movie."

"*What movie is it?*"

"A Gangster's Melody. Why?"

"I seen it already you gonna hate the ending. I'm on my way, be outside."

"OMG. What about Monica?"

"You know I don't like that bitch anyway, figure it out."

"Okay, okay."

"Hurry up," he said and hung up the phone.

Monica was so wrapped up into the movie she didn't even hear the convo. I knew I was going to hear her mouth, but fuck it.

"Hey" I said, nudging her.

"Bye bitch. I heard the whole thing. I'll see you later. Be careful," she replied never taking her eyes off the screen.

"Oh shit. You ain't mad?"

"No. Now shut the hell up, you making me miss the movie."

"Okay girl, I'll see you later," I whispered as I eased by her.

I was only outside a few seconds before Bruno pulled up. I opened the door and got in. He had a stoic look on his face as he stared straight ahead not even acknowledging me.

"Okay babe. What's so important that I had to leave the movie?" I asked.

Without warning he backhanded me across the face, causing my head to hit the passenger's side window. This was no dream, the situation was real and the pain was real. My vision was blurry and everything was moving in slow motion. It seemed like forever before his hand was back on the wheel. I had never been hit in the face before. My parents never did it, let alone a nigga. I was shocked and afraid. I wanted to cry, but that would ruin the façade that I had built up. I fought back the tears so hard that it hurt my eyes and gave me a headache out of this world. I toughened up and played my role.

"What the fuck was that for?" I screamed.

"Because bitch. Listening to you got my nephew killed. I should hit your fucking ass again."

Now that he was looking at me, I could see that he was geeked out of his mind. His eyes were bloodshot red and the rim of his nose was wet from previous running.

"What? I don't even know what you're talking about."

He hit me again, a little harder this time. My cheek felt like somebody had taken a lit match to it.

"Baby wait. What is going on? And why are you hitting me? " I questioned as a tear forced its way out of my eye.

"You told me to bring it to that nigga Travon and that's what I did. I tried to set him up for six more bricks. I sent my nephew to catch the lick and he got his fuckin' head blown off," he screamed as he hit me once more.

Now I was mad. As we approached a red light, Bruno slowed the car down and brought it to a halt. He attempted to say something...

"None of this would've happened if ..."

I balled up my fist and with all my might; I punched that motherfucker right on the bridge of his nose, which immediately caused his eyes to water up. Then I took my other fist and caught him in his jaw. That was a trick my daddy taught me. Before Bruno could gather himself I took his gun out of his waistband and stuck the barrel under his chin.

"Bitch is you crazy?" he said obviously in shock from the attack.

"Yeah motherfucker, and you about to see just how crazy I am. Don't worry though; I'll make sure to have the car detailed so they can get the brain fragments out," I stated trying to sound tough as I cocked the hammer back.

"Okay, Okay Ma, chill the fuck out. I'm sorry. I just lost it. Now stop before that shit goes off accidentally," he pleaded with his bitch ass.

"Oh nigga if it goes off, it won't be by accident trust me. Consider yourself warned; now drive motherfucker the lights green."

"Okay Ma, give me the heater," he replied sticking his hand out.

"No thank you. I'll hold onto this, until you get your mind right."

He chuckled a little and pulled off.

When we got back to his apartment, he filled me in on exactly what happened. It was a stupid move; even I knew that, but I wouldn't tell him that. Instead I pretended to console him and give a fuck about what he was going through.

"Babe it will be okay. I don't want to sound insensitive, but this is the life that was chosen," I said, rubbing his shoulders.

"What the fuck did you just say to me? My little nephew is dead. How the fuck am I gonna look my sister in the face ever again knowing that I'm responsible for having her son getting stretched out?"

"But baby, this is what I'm talking about. All I'm saying is, when you sent him out there, you had to factor in the possibility that he might not make it back," I said sounding like I knew the game, but really using common sense.

"Yeah I feel you, but I'm stuck like what the fuck am I supposed to do now? I made a move and I fucking blew it. Now I got my soldiers and everybody in the projects looking at me, waiting on my next move."

Bruno took an inhaler full of coke out of his pocket and two large snorts, one in each nostril. He shook his head hard, feeling the effects.

"Baby maybe you should slow down," I suggested pretending to care, but the truth of the matter was really that I had him right where I wanted him and I couldn't afford to have him overdose.

"I'm good Tiff. Just need a little something to help me get my mind right, that's all," he replied rubbing his nose.

"That's what you got me here for," I said stroking his chin and his ego at the same time.

"I know. That's why you can't go no-where. You can forget about Baltimore for now."

"What? No Bruno. I can't stay here."

"Look. You said every successful king needs a strong queen by his side during times of war, and as of today we are at defcon red."

"Bruno I feel you, but I ain't trying to just be your pretty girl trophy piece. If we are going to do this, we are going to do it together," I stated hoping that I didn't overplay my hand.

"No doubt. Ain't no turning back now. I just gotta figure out what my next move is."

"That's simple. Travon took one of your people, so you take three of his. Fuck it."

"Damn Tiffany, you are one devious bitch and I like it. The only problem is, that nigga Travon is like a ghost. Sometimes you see him, but most times you don't. Nobody even knows where he lives at."

"Okay, well if you can't get to him, get to his people. Go to his hangouts. He don't live under a rock babe."

"Yeah you right. I'm gonna have to do some research, because up until now; I ain't never gave a fuck about that niggas life."

"What about his club. Why don't you get at him there?"

"Yeah that's a thought, but shit, security in that motherfucker is tighter than fish pussy and they be surrounding that nigga like he's Obama or some shit."

"Yeah Bruno, but you gotta be able to catch him going in, or coming out of the club."

"Hmm, that might be a possibility. Hold up. How do you know he owns a club?"

Oh shit. I fucked up. Think Tiffany. Think. Shit. Damn. Fuck!

"Oh. I didn't know he owned a club. I just figured he had a club that he frequented a lot, most cats with that long bread do," I said confidently hoping my bullshit worked.

"Oh okay. Yeah his bitch ass owns a club. I used to go there all the time."

"Well you're gonna have to figure something out quick. If this Travon guy has any sense, he's gonna come at you with everything he's got."

"Well I'm not hiding, that's for damn sure."

"And you shouldn't. Why would that even be a thought?"

"I never said it was a thought, but this shit is gonna get real bloody, really fast. That niggas squad is deep."

Ugh. His bitch-assness was pissing me off!!!

"So what. You have a whole housing project that you control. You better start doing some recruiting and get your numbers up. Now you say dude ran off with four keys, and your nephew missed the attempt for the six, so what are you doing as far as product is concerned?"

"I took a couple dollars and hollered at my man out in Newark. His shit ain't nowhere near as good as Travon's shit, but it's good enough to get me by until I figure things out."

"Good job baby. Look Bruno, you got this. I believe in you. This shit is yours for the taking. Go get it and destroy anybody in your way," I said kissing softly him on the lips.

"Damn. I been looking for a rider like you for a long time," he said stuck in my gaze like a deer in the headlights.

"Well you got one now, don't blow it."

IT'S OFFICIAL

I got back to the hotel and dreaded having the conversation with Monica about Bruno wanting me to stay and move in with him. When I opened the door she was in the living room watching television.

"Well, well, well. Look what the cat drug in," she said sarcastically.

"Oh whatever Monica," I responded putting my pocketbook down and plopping down on the couch across from her.

"Bitch what the fuck happened to your face?" she snapped as she jumped up off the couch.

I hadn't even checked my face since last night's fiasco. When I washed it this morning it still hurt, but I was half sleep and the bathroom light was off.

"Oh um, it ain't shit," I said feeling stupid as hell.

"What the fuck you mean it ain't shit? That motherfucker put his hands on you? Oh it is fucking on now," she screamed.

"Calm down Monica. Listen to me. Don't worry about my face, the plan is working great."

"What? Did he knock your damn brains loose? Was your plan to get your ass whooped? If it was, it seems to be working just fine."

"Look Monica. All this means is that I'm in good with him now. I'm in so good, that he asked me to stay and move in with him. Him and Travon are beefing heavy and I'm pulling Bruno's strings at will. This shit is easier than I thought it. You go on back to Baltimore. This shit will be over soon and I'll be back kicking it with you as if nothing ever happened." I stated trying to sound re-assuring.

"You have really lost your damn mind. At first I thought you were just talking out ya ass and venting, but now I see you are so focused on this revenge shit that you really don't care if you get yourself hurt or killed. Are you that drunk with revenge?" she yelled.

"You god damn right I am. I can't believe you thought I was bluffing. Oh I get it. You thought you was still fucking with the dumb, naïve ass Tiffany, fresh off the Greyhound from nowhere huh? Nah baby girl, this is a whole new Tiffany. I sat in that fucking cell four long ass years, thinking I would never see the outside of them walls again, but I swore that if by chance I did; I would make that motherfucker Travon pay or I would die trying. You have the nerves to ask me if am I drunk with revenge? Well my answer to you is, you're motherfucking right, so you go on back home and don't worry about me. I'm good," I said as I broke down crying.

Monica came over, sat next to me and hugged me tightly, as I cried uncontrollably.

"It's gonna be okay," she said as she rocked me back and forth.

"That motherfucker gotta pay Monica. He gotta fucking pay for what he did to me."

"Okay, okay. If you're sure that this is what you want to do, who am I to stop you?"

"Thank you Monica. I know you're trying to look out for my best interest, but this is something that I have to do."

"I feel you, but I wouldn't be your girl if I left you here by yourself, so I'm gonna ask my boo if I can stay a while longer."

"That's why you my bitch," I sniffled.

"Yeah yeah. I realize you grown now and you ain't the same young chick I took under my wing years ago. So I'm gonna let you handle your business. Just be careful. If you get yourself killed, I'm gonna fuck you up."

"Uh. I can assure you that is not part of the plan," I said as I smiled through my tears.

"I love you girl."

"I love you too."

HIDE

Over the next few weeks, I was trying to get used to being Bruno's live in bitch. Pretending that I gave a fuck about his punk ass was becoming tiresome. It was now evident that by crossing Travon, Bruno had stepped way out of his league and he knew it. I'm sure that he regretted what he did, but it was too late to turn back now. Bruno had become paranoid and his constant use of coke only heightened his sense of paranoia. He was constantly looking out of the window, checking and double-checking before he went outside. For the first few days I wasn't even allowed to leave the apartment. I felt like a prisoner. I would have to wait for Bruno to fall asleep or make a quick run just so I could sneak out and go to the corner store. He was so afraid to go out that he wouldn't check on his workers for days at a time. Today, like most days; he sat around with no shave, or haircut playing X-Box and sniffing coke. He wasn't bringing no money in and I was tired of spending my own. Enough was enough.

"Bruno," I said as he sat there playing the game in his New York Knicks basketball shorts and wife beater.

"Yeah, what up?" he responded not taking his eyes off the video game.

"I'm tired of being cooped up in this apartment. I'm going crazy. I need to get out of here for a while."

"Come on. We already been through this, until the heat dies down we gotta lay low."

"Uh excuse me, but I'm not the one with the heat, so why do I have to suffer?"

"We in this together remember? So sit back and relax, it will all be over soon."

"How in the hell is it gonna be over soon and your ass in here doing nothing but getting high and playing fucking video games all day every day? Look at you, no shave, no haircut, did you even wash ya ass today?"

He paused the game.

"Bitch don't play yourself. You think what I'm going through is easy? You try looking over your shoulder everywhere you go. You try living with the fact that you know you got in way over your head and a nigga can split your shit at any given moment. You try living like that and then judge me." He snarled.

"Baby, I'm not judging you. I'm simply saying being tucked away in the house ain't solving the problem. You think if you just chill for a few weeks, everything is just going to blow over? I highly doubt that."

"So what do you suggest I do? Do you know how hard it is going to war with a ghost? How the hell am I supposed to kill something I can't fucking catch?"

"That's just it, you're going about it all wrong. You don't go looking for him. You make him come looking for you. Dangle a little bait out, and when he shows his face, then you take it off. I understand your worries, but like I said before; this is the life you chose. You got a lot of people depending on you. You have an organization to run and you are losing money every day that you are not out there handling your business."

"That's what I got Mikey for. His job is to hold shit down for me when I can't do it."

"It's not that you can't do it, you won't do it, and Mikey's ya boy and shit, but I don't think you should let him be portrayed as the man for too long. Power is a motherfucker and sometimes it's hard to give back once you've tasted it. Prime example, he hasn't called you with the count in four days. That type of protocol would never have been broken if you were on point and running shit the way you usually do."

"Yeah, you right about that, and you know what Ma? I have been tripping. Money, bitches, bullets and jail all come with the territory, so fuck it; it is what it is."

"Exactly, but the only thing on that list you should be worried about is the money, none of that other shit matters. The object of the game is not to just make money, but to also live long enough to enjoy it. Now pull yourself together and go handle your business."

"You dead right Ma. Fuck it," he said as he pulled out his nose candy inhaler.

I grabbed his hand.

"You should really lay off that shit too. You need to be on point out there in them streets."

"Trust me. This does keep me on point. It keeps me aware and alert at all times," he said pulling his bulletproof vest out of the hall closet and putting it on.

"So where you going?" I asked.

"First I'm going to the barber shop and then I'm going to Baisley and set shit straight," he replied putting his shirt and jacket on over his vest.

"Okay babe, you be careful out there. I'll call you and check on you while I'm out and about."

"Out and about? Who said you was going anywhere?"

"Come on Bruno, don't start that shit again. I'm gonna call Monica and have her pick me up for some shopping. It's been awhile since I last spent some time hanging with Monica. I kind of miss my girl."

"Look. Don't be out all day, and you know the drill. Don't have her come to the house. You catch a cab and meet her somewhere," he replied with his paranoid ass.

"Okay Bruno damn. Well give me some money then so I can do some shopping please," I said with my hand out.

He dug in his pocket and removed a medium sized wad of money. He counted out five hundred dollars and attempted to put the rest back in his pocket. I took the wad out of his hand, leaving him with the five hundred.

"Nigga you know better," I said as I headed into the bedroom to get dressed.

Bruno followed behind me and picked his gun off the dresser and put it in his waistband. Then he put on one of his chains, kissed me on the cheek and left.

I immediately called Monica to set up our rendezvous. She gave me a time and place and I hung up to get ready.

SEEK

Once I got in my car, I called my barber Mr. Teddy. He was an old head who had been cutting my hair since I was a kid. I was so young that my mother used to send me with a note telling him how to cut my hair. Mr. Teddy was what you would call a pillar in the community. My usual day to get my cuts was on Tuesdays, but shit changed with all this drama going on. I told him I was in desperate need of a cut and I was on my way in.

On the way to the shop I had some time to think about the situation that I had gotten myself into. I guess at the end of the day, it was a necessary evil. Once those bricks came up missing I knew there would no reasoning with that nigga Travon, so going at him was really my only option. My ego was kind of bruised. It took Tiffany to put things into perspective for me in order for me to make this power move. It cost my nephew his life, but she was right; this was the life we chose. Tiffany was thorough as fuck and I could see us really going places. She was beautiful, intelligent and well rounded. She was definitely a keeper.

I pulled up in front of the barbershop and parked my car. I got out, hit the alarm and strolled inside.

"Heeeey, what's up stranger?" Mr. Teddy said as he spun the chair around, about to take the clippers to the little boy's head that was sitting in the chair.

"What's up Mr. Teddy? How is everything?" I asked giving him dap and a hug.

"Well you know Bruno, trying to maintain, that's all you can do now a days. Of course you'd know that if you kept your appointments. I ain't seen you in over two weeks."

"Yeah I know Mr. Teddy, I been out of town," I lied knowing damn well that I had been laying low and getting my hair cut had not been a top priority for me until Tiffany got into my ass about looking like shit.

"You stay on the move, I'll tell you that much."

"Yeah and speaking of which, I'm kind of in a rush right now. Is there any way I can jump in front of little man?"

"Well I ain't started on him yet, but you gonna have to take that up with his mama," he said nodding in the direction of shorty's moms.

She was a bad ass brown skinned chick, with beautiful brown eyes with a body that look like she stayed away from junk food. She had on a form fitting BCBG sweat suit and some Louis sneakers.

"Don't even think about it. I'm in a rush too, so unfortunately you gonna have to wait your turn," she said smiling, but meaning every word of it.

"Mr. Teddy let me borrow this for a minute," I said as I grabbed a pen out of his shirt pocket. I then pulled a hundred dollar bill out of my pocket and wrote my name and number on it and handed it to her.

"Here you go pretty. This should cover your inconvenience," I said.

"Uh no thank you. I have my own money sweetie, but if it's that important to you then go ahead. Come on Jermaine, get down and let the man go first," she said handing me back the money.

"Thanks Ma, I appreciate it. Here you go little man. Go play some video games until it's your turn," I said attempting to hand him a dollar bill. He looked at his mother for her approval. She nodded her head, and he took the money and ran to the back to play the games.

"Thanks again," I said winking at her.

"Just hurry up." She joked.

I sat down in the chair and Mr. Teddy spun me around away from the front of the shop facing the mirror. He cut my hair as we talked about old times and the old neighborhood. Then Mr. Teddy stopped cutting.

"Hold up Bruno. Old Mr. Teddy gotta run to the bathroom. You know my bladder ain't what it used to be."

"I can dig it Mr. Teddy, go ahead."

He spun my chair around facing the window and scurried off to the bathroom.

"Now you can't blame me for being late for your appointment, you gotta blame Mr. Teddy," I joked.

"Uh huh. Whatever," she replied.

"So what's your name pretty?"

201

"Jasmine and yours?"

I was about to respond, but was interrupted my cell phone alerting me to an incoming text. It was from an unfamiliar number. I hit the button to open the message and it read:

"GOTCHU MOTHERFUCKER!"

Before I could process the message, gunshots rang out and penetrated the barbershop window, sending shards of glass flying everywhere. Jasmine screamed and ran to protect her son, while I was pinned down by what felt like four shots to the chest. My chest felt like it was hit with a wrecking ball. The force of the multiple large caliber bullets knocked the wind out of me. I imagined that the gunmen fled because I never heard the jingling bells of the shop's door opening and I heard a car's tires peel off. I lay there in pain with my eyes closed. I heard jasmine screaming hysterically as little man cried from fear. Mr. Teddy ran from the back and held my head in his arms.

"Got dammit, got dammit. Noooooooo!" he screamed.

"I'm so sorry young blood. They said they just wanted to talk to you. I didn't know this would happen. God please forgive me. They said I would never see my family again," he cried.

"And you still won't," I said, as I opened my eyes, took my 9mm out, put it in his mouth and pulled the trigger.

I hopped out the chair and quickly hobbled up over to Jasmine and her son who were cowering in the corner.

"Were you in here today?" I asked with my gun pointed at her.

"What?" she said covering her son and shaking hysterically.

I cocked the gun and put it to her son's head.

"Bitch I said did you come in this motherfucker today?"

"Noooo, nooooo. Please don't. I wasn't here. I never came in here today."

"I grabbed my chest in pain and backed away.

"Good job Ma. Good job," I said as I turned and left.

I jumped in my car and peeled off, as I heard police sirens in the distance. I gunned my whip towards the expressway headed for Baisley. Once I was far enough away, I pulled over to the shoulder and took off my jacket and shirt. There were four large slugs embedded in my vest. I removed the vest and lifted my wife beater to see that my chest was black and blue from the impact of the bullets. I put my shirt back on and pulled off again. I immediately called Mikey. The phone rang twice before he picked up.

"*What up Bee?*" he answered nonchalantly.

"Yo strap up. That nigga Travon just tried to have me murked."

"*What? Where nigga? What happened?*"

"I was at getting my haircut and Mr. Teddy set me up. Motherfuckers sent shots through the shop window."

"*Oh shit. You a'ight son?*"

"Yeah. I took four in the chest, but I was vested up."

"Damn that's crazy. I can't believe Mr. Teddy set you up. Did you check the old head?"

"Let's just say. He won't get another shot at it. Anyway I'm on my way to you. Have everybody meet me at Miss Tracy's house in twenty minutes."

"*Okay bet.*"

"Yo. I need you to put the take from the last four days in a duffle bag and bring it with you."

"*Shit Bee. You don't need a duffle bag. You can fit all that shit in your pockets.*"

"What? What the fuck is you talking about Mikey?" I screamed.

"*Yo God, shit been crazy out here in these streets. Travon got niggas shook. So they ain't tryna' get caught outside.*"

"Are you fucking serious? What kind of niggas you got on our team Mikey?"

"Come on son. You know our team is thorough as fuck, that's why they been down with us for years, but in they defense; this is a whole new ballgame we playing."

"Well I'm about to bench a lot of motherfuckers. I'm on my way," I said ending the call and throwing the cell phone down on the passenger's seat.

Miss Tracy was like the matriarch of the projects. As far as she was concerned, we were all her children, she held us down, and we took very good care of her. When I got to her apartment I knocked twice, once, and then twice again. The peephole slid open and then she opened the door.

"Hey Miss Tracy," I said kissing her on the cheek.

"Hello baby, how you been?" she said hugging me.

"I'm hanging in there, trying to maintain."

"I'm sorry to hear about your nephew."

"Yeah that shit is crazy."

"Boy, you better watch your mouth," she said slapping me on my arm.

"I'm sorry Miss Tracy."

"Mmm hmmm. Well get on in the back. Your friends are waiting for you. Ya'll want something to eat?"

"No Ma'am. We're fine, thank you," I answered as I headed to the back room.

When I got back there, Mikey and a few of the soldiers sat around the poker table that was used for Saturday night card games.

"What's good?" I asked rhetorically.

"Here you go my Gee," Mikey said handing me a few bundles of money wrapped in rubber bands.

"What's the count?"

"A little over twenty-one thousand," he replied reluctantly.

"Twenty-one thousand for four days worth of work? Are you fucking serious? I wipe my ass with twenty-one stacks," I yelled, as I threw the money up against the wall, causing the bills to scatter everywhere.

"Ya'll niggas scared to get this money all of a sudden? Oh. I get it. Shit ain't sweet no more, and now ya gotta work for it, ya'll niggas is showing your true colors. Well this shit right here is what real soldiering is about," I said lifting my shirt and exposing the black and blue impact bruises from the assignation attempt.

"This is what we get paid for. Now if ya'll can't handle earning your keep then get the fuck out now," I said seething and scanning the room.

Everyone stayed silent as I continued my tirade.

"Now, I want motherfuckers strapped up and working these projects around the clock. You see somebody that ain't from around here; you send something hot their way early. I ain't playing with ya'll niggas no more. I want no less than fifty grand per nigga, per shift. Anything less than that will not be tolerated. Mikey I want a squad of niggas laying outside of that nigga Travon's club. I want him followed, I wanna know where he eats, sleeps, and shits. This shit just got real and it will probably get worse before it gets better. Now get out there and make it happen. And if any of ya'll niggas bitch up, you ain't gotta worry about Travon dealing with you, I'll kill you myself. Mikey pick up this money, give Miss Tracy a stack and bring the rest to me."

"No doubt Bee. I'm on it."

I left the room and headed to the front of the apartment. Miss Tracy was in the living room watching Oprah.

"Thanks Miss Tracy. Mikey has something for you."

"Okay now. You be careful out there."

"Always," I said as I left the apartment.

IN TOO DEEP

"Baby are you okay?" I said observing the damage done to Bruno's chest.

"Yeah I'm good. Just to think, I almost walked out with my vest this morning."

"Okay baby look. Maybe I was wrong. Maybe you should just pull out of this mess you are in?" I lied pretending that I gave a fuck.

"What? No I'm all in now. It's an eye for an eye with that motherfucker. He has got to go, by any means necessary."

"I just don't want to see anything happen to you."

"Don't worry. I'll be good. I'm going to win this shit. I'm not even the slightest bit concerned."

"Well then maybe you should just lay low for a while. Let your team handle it for you."

"Nah. They need me to lead by example, so that's what I'm gonna do, besides I wanna be there when that motherfucker takes his last breath."

"Okay Bae. So what's the plan when you finally get rid of this dude?"

"Well hopefully I can figure out who his connect is first. If that happens, then I pick up where he left off at and all his customers will have to come and see me."

"And if you can't figure out the connect?"

"Then I'll use my Newark connect and they will still have to see me. I just wish I could get more info out of that nigga Travon before I bury his ass."

"Bruno think hard. There has got to be a weak link in his crew somewhere."

"Nah. Not in that niggas crew. They worship him like they worship Jesus."

"Okay, well what about at his club. Is there somebody there that can get close to him?"

"I don't know Tiffany. I ain't hire them motherfuckers at his club. I told you I don't know too much about him or his club. All I know is the nigga gets money, and I hear that he takes chicks up in his office at the club and breaks them off when he feels like it."

"Hmmm. So maybe that's your ticket. If you can plant a chick up in there and she can get in that office she might be able to find something."

"Tiffany that's gonna be tough. Plus these silly hoes I fuck with ain't built like that. They'll fuck the whole thing up."

"Oh well, it was just a suggestion."

"Wait. You could pull it off. You got the brains, the hustle, and I know that nigga Travon will be all over you."

I almost threw up in my mouth from the instant case of nausea.

"Huh? Me? No baby that wouldn't work," I stuttered.

"What do you mean? You're perfect. I know for a fact that you can work your way into that office, and once you're inside you are going to know exactly what to look for."

"Bruno that would more than likely mean that I would have to sleep with him and I know you don't want that."

"Look I don't give a fuck what you gotta do. Just get in there and do it. Now you said you was my rider and you was down for whatever. So this is what it has to be."

"Okay Bruno, I'll do it, but I think you should wait a few weeks. With everything that's going on right now he will smell a set up coming."

"You're right. I will let you know when the time is right. We'll talk more about it when I get back."

"Where you going baby? Don't you think you should rest?"

"Nah. I'm going to see my Moms. I'm gonna spend some time with her. I'll see you later."

He kissed me on the lips and walked out of the door.

PREPARING FOR A NEW LIFE

"Okay Monica, things are moving a lot quicker than planned. So we gonna have to alter the plans a little bit."

"Alter them how baby? We still leaving ain't we?"

"Of course we are, but it may be sooner than we expected."

"How soon?"

"Shit. The way things are looking, real soon. You remember the plan right?"

"Yes baby, we've been over it a thousand times."

"Okay well I know Miami was the original get a way spot, but something tells me that's not going to be far enough away, so I want you to go down to the Bahamas for a while and set things up the way we originally planned for Miami."

"Ooohh baby for real? I always dreamed of going there."

"Yeah well ya boo made it a reality for you."

"When do you want me to leave?"

"In a day or two."

"Okay baby. I'm so excited."

211

"Yeah well, I hate to ruin the mood, but who's gonna babysit Tiffany's ass while you're gone?"

"Oh baby didn't I tell you? She's heading back to Maryland any day now. She will probably leave the day I fly out now that this has come up."

"I don't care where she goes. Do not leave her ass here in New York. Do you understand me?"

"Yes baby I got you."

"Good. Now come on over here and put your mouth where I like it."

"Say no more baby."

IT ALL ADDS UP

I was in the house with Bruno and hating every minute of it. Today he was higher than I had ever seen him. His behavior was erratic and his paranoia was at an all time high.

"Look Tiff. I know we said we was gonna wait a while before we sent you up in that niggas club, but we gonna have to do that shit ASAP. I got my boys sitting on the club, and these dumb ass niggas follow him and keep losing him. I can't keep hiding I mean holding up in this apartment. We gotta put an end to this shit now."

"Bruno, I keep telling you that I don't think now is the time."

"Bitch I ain't ask you to think. I told your ass to do something."

"Baby listen…"

I was saved by Monica calling my cell.

"Hold on babe. It's Monica."

"Man fuck that bitch."

"Stop it babe. Hey girl what's up?" I said, answering the phone.

"Girl me and my boo are going on vacation."

"Aww that's what's up. When you leaving?"

213

"Tomorrow. I'm gonna leave my car with you while I'm gone so you ain't gotta keep catching cabs and shit. Plus I know you don't wanna drive that nigga Bruno's car with all the shit that he's into."

"You know that's right. Shit is crazy girl."

"Yeah well, you asked for it."

"Shut up bitch. So when am I gonna meet this boo of yours? This nigga must be butt ass ugly because you keeping him in the cut."

"Never that hoe, and what I tell you about being all in my business? Don't worry about who I'm fucking over here. You just worry about that lame ass nigga sticking dick to you over there.

"You know Monica, enough is enough show me this dude already. This mystery game is getting old now."

"It wouldn't be a mystery if you would just mind your damn business. Shit, since when do I have to report anything to you?"

"Oh it's like that now?"

"Like what? I'm just saying stop pressing me about who I'm fucking. It ain't even that serious damn."

"You know what. You're right. If that's how it is, then fuck it."

"Oh bitch stop crying. Like I said it ain't that serious. Oh by the way, I'm gonna need you to take me to the airport tomorrow and just keep the car till I get back."

"Wait a minute. I thought you was going with ya boo?"

"Oh, were gonna meet up out there in a few days. There are some loose ends that need be to tie up out here."

214

"Oh okay, so what time you want me to pick you up?"

"Well my flight leaves at 10am so I need to be at the JFK no later than 8:30am."

"Damn bitch that's early, but okay umm where am I taking a cab to bitch. Don't nobody know where you and secret squirrel stay at."

"Oh yeah. Shut up. Bruno's ass don't want nobody over there either. Just take the cab to the airport and meet me at the Delta check in terminal. I'll give you the keys there."

"Oh my god. I'm not doing all of that. I'll call you in the morning and tell you were to pick me up from."

"Don't make me late bitch. Bye."

I hung up the phone and turned to Bruno who was taking another bump of coke to the face.

"Baby Monica's leaving town in the morning, so I'm going to hold her car down while she's gone."

"Wherever she going, she needs to stay the fuck there," he said taking another bump.

"Baby leave my friend alone."

"Whatever. Anyway back to what I was saying, you get ready to go up in that club in the next day or so. We ain't got time to wait on this shit."

"Okay babe. Okay."

The next morning Bruno was sound asleep, so I text Monica and gave her the address to the house for the first time. I told her to text me back when she was pulling up and not to blow the horn. In about half hour she pulled up and did like she was told. I grabbed the house keys and tip toed out. I got in the car and gave her a hug.

"What's up girl?" I said.

"Ain't shit. No wonder you ain't wanna give me the address. That nigga live in this hole in the wall?" she said turning her nose up.

"Look it ain't my doing. Fuck him and his place. Now come on before you miss your plane and blame it on me."

"You already know. Got me going out the fucking way to pick your ass up."

"Oh shut up, put on that new Rick Ross CD and drive," I joked.

When we got to the airport she pulled up to the domestic departure at Delta. She popped the trunk and waived over a skycap. I got out and watched as they all stumbled over each other to get to her. Once her bags were secure on the luggage cart she tipped the guy fifty dollars as he wheeled her Louis luggage away.

"Now you take care of my baby. I would tell you to take care of yourself, but your hard headed ass ain't going to listen," She said giving me a kiss and a hug.

"Oh hush. Your baby and me will be just fine. You just have a good time and bring me something back besides stories bitch."

"You already know. I'll call you, and oh yeah nothing but premium gas goes into my princess."

"At these prices?" I joked

"Bitch you got it. Shut up."

"Okay, well let me get going before the warden wakes up."

"Yeah you do that, meanwhile I have to get in here before I miss my flight. You know they damn near strip search you and shit now."

"Yeah well, they should have fun with that."

"Bye bitch," she said laughing as she made her way into the terminal.

I got in the car and waited to make sure Monica was good. Since I have the worst sense of direction, I cycled through the recent destination list on her GPS. While trying to find Bruno's address, I constantly ran across an address that said *T's House*. It was a Long Island address, so I figured it must be where she has been shacking up with her mystery boo. For the life of me I could not figure out why she was being so secretive about this dude. The GPS said the address was only twenty-six minutes away. Curiosity and pure fact that I was just plain nosey got the best of me and I chartered a course straight for the address. I really needed to see what the big deal secret was; besides God forbid something happened to Monica, I needed to know where to look for answers, I tried to rationalize with myself.

I weaved in an out of the traffic on the Long Island Expressway as the GPS gave me step-by-step directions to my destination. I took the exit, along the twists and turns through the upscale neighborhood as I was instructed. One thing's for sure; whomever she was fucking had major paper to be living out here. These houses were like mini-mansions. I was admiring the houses, beautiful landscaping, and exotic cars when my thoughts were interrupted by the GPS. *In 400 yards your destination will be on the left.*

As I shortened the gap between the final destination, and myself I could see a man playing with his son in the yard. I quickly imagined my husband doing that with my children someday. A husband and children is something that I have always yearned for. *In 200 yards your destination will be on the left* the GPS reminded me. Suddenly my heart jumped into my throat and I immediately pulled the car over about five houses away, as I watched that motherfucker Travon Outlaw wrestle with his son on the front lawn. I was immediately engulfed in rage for a number of reasons. Number one, I was staring at my first love, my first lover, the only man I have ever given my heart to, the one who set me up and sent me to rot in jail forever, the one who caused the death of the unborn child that he fathered. Now here he was living happily ever after, enjoying a nice home with his family. My second siege of rage came from the fact that, not only was this motherfucker living the grand old life, but he was also fucking my so-called best friend; the only person on God's green earth that I trusted. He was a typical nigga, so I learned a little too late that his actions were common, but Monica, she was my sister. How the fuck could she do this to me? How could this betrayal be happening to me again? My heart started palpitating uncontrollably and it got even worse as I watched this motherfucker's wife come out of the house and kiss him the way I used to. It took everything in my not to put the car in drive and mow them down right where they stood. I began to cry hysterically as I realized that life, as I knew it was officially over. Monica was all that I had left and now she was dead to me too. I cried so much that my vision became blurred, my thoughts became cloudy, and I was no longer aware of anything that was going on around me. I attempted to mentally take myself to another place. A place where I could be alone and no one could ever hurt me again. A tap on the window from a little old white lady walking her poodle startled me. I reluctantly rolled the window down.

"Are you okay young lady? You have been here crying your eyes out for quite some time now."

"I'm fine thank you," I said noticing that the Outlaws were no longer outside. I put the car in drive and pulled off.

As I passed the house I almost threw up in my mouth as I saw silhouettes of the proud family through the window. I tried to gather myself as I reset the GPS to take me back to Bruno's. I hit the parkway and suddenly something happened. My hurt and pain turned into anger and vengeance. If motherfuckers wanted to play this game, I would hit the reset button, start the game over and even the playing field. From here on out, it was no holds bar and now that bitch Monica would have to feel my wrath too. I was going to fix the game so that I was the only winner. There would be no extra lives won after scoring 10,000 points. You only had one life and your job was to protect it at all times. Game on!

Just as I was formulating my plan, Bruno called my cell. I had never been so happy to see that lame ass niggas name and number come across my screen.

"Hello?"

"Yo, where the fuck you at?"

"I'm on my way home Bruno. Why?"

"Tonight is the night I want you up in that nigga Travon's club. I can't sit around waiting any longer. We got to make it happen tonight."

"Fall back babe. I can do you one better than that."

"What? What are you talking about Tiffany?"

"I got the motherfucker's home address. Not no stash house, not no flop house, it's his home, where he lays his head at with his wife and kids," I stated proudly.

"Get the fuck out of here. Say word. How you know the info is legit?"

"Just take my word for it. I wouldn't tell you about it unless I was sure," I responded, dancing around the question.

"Damn that's what's up? Where you get the info from?"

"Well let's just say, my girl Monica ain't the best friend she's cracked up to be."

"See. I told you that bitch had some shit with her."

"Come on Bruno. Ain't nobody got time for that I told you so bullshit. Try wrapping your stupid ass mind around the fact that I'm gonna have to check someone I thought was very close to my heart when she gets back," I snapped, starting to tear up again.

"You want me to handle that bitch for you?"

"Shut the fuck up. Bye Bruno."

I threw the phone down and headed for his house. I was mentally at the point of no return, and emotionally at the point of no longer giving a fuck.

BITE THE BULLET

I was doing a hundred miles per hour headed towards home. Janelle had called and was screaming hysterically about the kids. She was crying and screaming so bad that I couldn't make out anything that she was saying. All I heard was kids and danger. That's all I needed to hear. No matter how I may be perceived on the outside, on the inside I was a family man, and I loved my kids to death. I pulled up in my driveway and ran into the house, where I found Janelle on the couch still crying; rocking my sons back and forth on the couch. When she saw me, she put the kids down, hurried over to me and slapped me across the face.

"What the fuck?" I yelled shocked.

"They came to our house and threatened our gotdamn kids," she screamed

"What? Who? What the hell are you talking about?"

"I don't fucking know. Whoever you done pissed off, they came to our home where our children lay their heads," she said pounding my chest with both hands until I grabbed her.

"Yo. Slow down, breath and start from the beginning. What the fuck happened?"

"Chris and TJ were playing out front and Chris says a black guy in a white truck drove up and asked if you was their father. When TJ said yes, the motherfucker told him to catch and threw him this Travon," she screamed, hitting me again and dropping an AK-47 round into my hand.

"He said to tell you that the next one is going to be coming a lot faster," she continued.

"Motherfucker! Pack the kids up and take them to your sister's house for a while," I yelled in anger.

"Travon, I know you know who's behind this shit. I want you to handle that shit accordingly. Do you hear me?"

"I got it Janelle."

"No Travon. I need you to make sure this never happens again," she said looking me dead in the eye.

"Okay baby, okay. I'm on it," I said kissing her and holding her in my arms.

"Protect our family Travon, but be careful. What would we do without you?"

"I'm going to be alright, we're going to be alright. Now I want you to get your .38 out of the closet and keep it with you at all times. If anybody besides the mailman or me come to that door, you do exactly what I taught you. You hear me?" I said holding her head up by her chin.

"Yes baby, I hear you."

"Okay lock the door. I'll be back later."

"Travon I love you baby, handle your business and come home."

"I promise to do both," I said walking over to hug and kiss my boys."

"Daddy loves ya'll. I'll be back in a little while and we can play the X-Box."

I gave Janelle a long passionate kiss, told her I loved her and left.

I jumped in my car seething with anger. I had to play it cool in front of the family, but now that I was alone I could show my true emotions.

"Fuck, fuck, fuck," I yelled pounding my fist against the steering wheel.

I calmed myself down long enough to call Lorenzo.

"What's good Tray? He said as he answered.

"Yo, that motherfucker Bruno brought the beef to my doorstep. That motherfucker threatened my kids.

"What? That nigga came to your crib? Yo, he has got to go. I told you to let me peel that nigga long time ago."

"Yeah well I was playing politics then, but it's a whole new ball game now. I want everybody at the club in an hour sharp. I don't want anybody late. It's time we bring Baisley down brick by brick.

"Finally. That's what I'm talking about. I'll make the calls now."

"Alright I'm on my way."

MARKED FOR DEATH

I was driving around trying to gather my thoughts. I had come to the conclusion that it was stupid of me to give Bruno Travon's address? For all I know Bruno's dumb ass could have went over there and shot Travon's house up with wife and kids inside. His wife and kids were innocent in all of this and I put them in harm's way. Bruno was being tight lipped about the situation, so I don't know what he did, if anything. I prayed to almighty God that he didn't harm those kids. In any event, tomorrow was my last day in New York. I was in way over my head, and depending on what Bruno did with that information I gave him, I could very well be an accessory to murder or some other shit.

Tonight I planned to hit Bruno up for the biggest slice of cake he ever gave me and in the morning I was taking Monica's car and putting New York in my rear view. I would go back to B-More, gather my things, and relocate. I had not yet decided what to do with Monica's bitch ass. It's just good for her that she wasn't around. Monica hurting me was the equivalent of Travon hurting me, maybe even worse. I would find a way to get her ass later, right now I needed to plan my escape from New York.

I was about to call Michelle and fill her in on the fuckery, but Bruno called first. I started to send his ass to voicemail, but decided against it. I needed to plant the seed in his head to get this bread from him.

"Hey baby," I said pretending to be excited about his call.

"What's good? Where you at?"

"I'm just cutting some corners and running some errands. Why what's up?"

"Meet me at the jaguar dealership in Manhattan that I took you to the other day."

"Babe, I'm all the way in Queens. I was just about to treat myself to some lunch."

"Just come on. I brought my car to get serviced and it's gonna take longer than I expected. I ain't trying to sit her for no two hours. I'll take you to lunch and we can go wherever you want, just as long as we're back by 4pm.

"We can eat anywhere I want?"

"Yeah that's my word."

"Okay. I'm on my way, and I hope you brought your large stacks because I'm starving."

"You already know. Now hurry up."

"Okay, okay," I said as I hung the phone up.

When I pulled up to the dealership Bruno was outside on his cell phone. He hung it up when he saw me. I parked the car and got out.

"What you doing? He asked

"You drive. I've been driving all morning."

"Yo, I ain't pushing that foul ass bitch's whip."

"Nigga you about to ride in it, so what's the difference?"

"Whatever. Just get in," he said adjusting the driver's seat.

We pulled off and I went right in on him.

"So baby I was thinking, with all this beefing going on, maybe we should relocate."

"What? You bugging. I ain't leaving New York are you crazy?"

"I ain't talking about leaving the state; I'm talking about finding a new crib. I was looking at some spots that were real nice, and they were in the cut. Nobody would know we were there," I lied.

"You was looking at some spots huh? You never cease to amaze me. You are always thinking one step ahead."

"Yeah well, I have to stay on point. I know you have a lot going on, and you can't think of everything."

"That's what's up. So it's a nice spot right?"

"Yeah. Three bedrooms, two and a half baths, eat in kitchen, two car garage, and a private finished basement so you can handle your business on the low."

"Say word. Where is it at?"

"Jamaica Estates."

"Yeah I always wanted to move out there. That's peace Ma. How much they want for the spot?"

"Well that's what I was afraid to tell you. It's kind of steep."

"Look. You can't put a price on safety or comfort. What's the ticket?"

"We need ten thousand five hundred dollars to move in. that will cover first and last month's rent plus the security deposit."

"Damn that shit is thirty five hundred dollars a month?"

"Yeah babe but trust me it's worth it, and don't worry I will put it in my name so there is no paper trail back to you. I know the rules."

"I trust your taste. Matter fact I ain't even taking none of that old ass furniture with us. We are going to buy all new shit. I'll give you the bread when we get back home. How soon can we move in, because we gonna have to get low really quick."

"The apartment is empty and ready to move into. So whenever we are ready I guess."

"Okay cool."

"Aww baby. Thank you. I can't wait."

"It's all good. We about to run this city, so why not live like it."

"Good answer."

We drove for a while in bumper-to-bumper traffic, when Bruno pulled the car over.

"What you doing babe?"

"This traffic is killing me. If we gonna be slow rolling I need to get my mind right. I'm running in that store to get a blunt."

"Really Bruno? You gonna drive through midtown Manhattan in broad daylight smoking weed? Are you serious?"

"As a heart attack," he said as he exited the car.

As a force of habit I started to text Monica to see what she was up to, but then quickly remembered that I now hated the bitch. Bruno came out of the store and in pure niggerish fashion opened the blunt and dumped the filling out onto the Manhattan sidewalk. He walked around the front of the car and opened the door.

"Tiffany I can't wait to roll this…"

Suddenly shots rang out Bruno was hit but I couldn't tell where.

"Tiff it's a hit," he yelled pulling his gun from his waist band and returning fire in every direction.

There was blood everywhere and bullets were piercing the car by the second. I could see people running for cover. I screamed and balled up against the passenger's side door as if that would protect me from the hail of bullets. Bruno was bleeding badly but continued to return fire, and then suddenly it was over. The last two shots I heard had slumped Bruno's lifeless body over the steering wheel and sent a burning sensation through my body that I would only feel for a few seconds before I closed my eyes.

When I opened my eyes, everything was white and I had finally joined my Mom and Dad.

DONE DEAL

When I got to the club, I immediately rushed up to my office where Shanise, Lorenzo, Sayeed and Jo Jo sat patiently awaiting my arrival.

"What's good babe? When do we make that bitch ass nigga Bruno take a dirt nap?" Shanise started.

"That's already taken care of," I said pouring myself a drink.

"What? What you do you mean it's already taken care of? Did you outsource the job to another crew?" Lorenzo asked.

"Nope, I handled that shit myself," I responded taking the drink to the head.

"What? How? When did you have time to do that? Sayeed joined in.

"I guess it was just a bad day for that motherfucker. On the way here I stopped to get gas and when I look up who do I see across the street getting into an S500?"

"Bruno? Get the fuck out of here? Jo Jo jumped in.

"Who was he with?" Shanise asked.

"He was by his motherfucking self. I swear, if it wasn't in the middle of Manhattan I would have walked over and spit on his dead body."

"Damn that's crazy. You sure he gone?" Jo Jo asked pouring himself a shot.

"I wet the whole fucking car up. Plus I finished him off with a headshot. That niggas a memory."

"Okay, so what's the next move?" Shanise asked, eagerly.

"We overthrow Baisley's government. Lorenzo, you and Jo Jo take as many hitters as we got on the payroll down to Baisley, find that nigga Mikey and tell him he just inherited half of Bruno's debt, and either he can get on board or the projects will have funerals every week; starting with his."

"Alright. Cool."

"Everybody else, it's back to business as usual. Ding dong the bitch is dead," I said raising my glass.

I was about to propose a toast, when Sophia called.

"Wassup Babe?"

"*Have you lost your fucking mind Travon?*" she screamed.

"What? Stop screaming. What are you talking about?"

"*A shoot out in broad daylight. Are you fucking serious?*"

"Okay so I cancelled that niggas contract, big deal. How did you find out so fast?"

"*Well when you turn midtown Manhattan into South Jamaica Queens in broad daylight news travels fast. Oh yeah, and the fact that you killed a ten-year old boy and left a young woman fighting for her life gives every news station something to talk about.*"

"Hold up. A ten-year-old boy dead? Some bitch in critical condition? I ain't got shit to do with that," I shouted defending myself.

"Actually you do Travon. The little boy was caught in the crossfire, and the girl was in the car with Bruno."

"Damn. Well dead men tells no tales, so how do they know it's me?"

"There are witnesses Travon. This is midtown Manhattan, not the hood. They could care less about that no snitching bullshit. They have your description and your license plate number. You really fucked yourself this time Travon. How could you be so fucking stupid?" she said sounding disappointed in me.

"Yo, when I saw that motherfucker I just snapped out. That nigga went to my home and threatened my kids."

"Travon you have been in the game long enough to know there is a time and a place for everything. That's how you have been able to operate all of these years without any issues, well except for the whole Baltimore fiasco which you escaped by the skin of your teeth."

"Witnesses huh? How much time do I have?" I asked looking at my watch.

"I'd say half hour tops. Maybe less. You're not thinking about running are you?"

"Running? Hell no, I got money. The D.A. will have to turn the witness list over to my attorney *when it comes down right?"*

"Yeah. Legally they have to why?"

"I'll have my people visit the witnesses, I'll pay them to lie, or they'll die. It's as simple as that."

"Travon are you willing to kill more people? Wasn't the death of Terri, Horse and D-Boy enough? Not to mention all the other bodies that you put in the ground."

"Look, like I told you before Terri was an accident, D-Boy deserved the bullet I gave him, and Horse, well that was just part of the game like everybody else."

"Travon I don't think…"

"Look, I don't pay you to think Sophia. Just do what the fuck I tell you to do," I barked.

"Well actually you do pay me to think, but okay have it your way. Them boys should be there shortly. Go quietly and don't give them a reason to shoot your dumb ass. You're probably going to be denied bail so I wouldn't look forward to it if I were you."

"You are going to be at the arraignment right?"

"I don't know Travon. I think you should use one of your other attorneys on this case. What you did today is going to bring down a ball of fire that even I can't douse. If they find out that you and I are involved, and they will if they dig, they'll have me removed from the case anyway. I can maneuver and try to pull strings for you behind the scenes, but I don't want to risk fucking your case up any more than it already is."

"Okay. I can dig it. I'll let my white boy Jeremy Eisenberg take care of it."

"I'm going to go and break the news to Janelle for you. Don't worry I got your back baby. We'll get through this."

"I know you do, and I know you will. Tell Janelle to wait on my call."

"Okay. Times ticking so get you and the squad cleaned up and I'll come clean up after ya'll when everybody is gone. Be careful. They're coming heavy and their mouths are watering."

"Cool. Thanks baby," I said as I hung up and turned to my squad who were eagerly hanging onto my every word.

"Okay I'm sure ya'll heard. Them boys are on the way so if your dirty, I suggest you get cleaned up now."

"Damn Tray. Shit is real like that?" Shanise asked.

"Apparently so. I fucked up, but it ain't about shit. We are not going to slow down or miss a beat. Everything will still go according as planned. Lorenzo is in charge while I'm gone. Ya'll give him the same respect and devotion you gave me. Renzo, you take care of my family while I'm gone, both of them."

"Oh you know that goes without saying my Gee," he replied.

"Tray we got company, and a lot of it," Sayeed said pointing to the video monitor.

We all directed our attention to the monitor, which showed what looked like the entire New York Police Department including the S.W.A.T. team with their weapons drawn. They converged on the club like they were U.S. troops storming the beaches of Normandy in WWII. My office door was triple locked again, so that would buy us some time, but not much. I rushed over to the bar and opened up a false panel in the back that I had built for just such an occasion. Inside the stash spot was a little over sixty seven thousand in cash, and the information to a safety deposit box that no one knew about.

"Okay, I thought we would have more time to get up out of here and get clean, but I guess this will have to do. Let's go, whatever you got that can get you booked; put it in here. I don't care what it is. I should be the only one leaving here for more than a few hours today," I instructed as I put my guns in the stash and watched as they all did the same.

Suddenly there were three loud bangs on the door.

"NYPD. Open this door."

I closed the stash and poured everybody a shot while pouring the usual triple for myself.

"Well this is it ya'll. Now I'll see what ya'll are made of when I'm not around. Let no law hold us down."

"Let no man bring us under," they all responded as we threw back our shots.

"Open this door now or we'll blow it open," the lead detective shouted.

I looked over at the monitor and watched as they brought a battering ram up the steps. I definitely didn't want them damaging my door so I walked over and unlocked the first and second locks, and before I could get the third lock completely unlocked the door flew open.

"Freeze. Everybody on the floor. Show me your fucking hands," they screamed as my squad waited for me to hit the floor before they followed suit. I loved my squad. They were the truth.

"Travon Outlaw, you are under arrest for the murders of ten-year old Billy Hatcher, twenty seven year old Dexter "Bruno" Miles, and twenty five year old Caprice Johnson," The lead detective stated as he cuffed me.

The rest of the squad was cuffed and hauled away too, but that was just protocol. If they had no warrants they would be released in a few hours. I on the other hand, was going to have to get used to being inconvenienced for a lot longer.

LONG LIVE THE KING

I had been on Rikers Island for a few weeks now and everything was going as planned. Lorenzo was running the squad flawlessly, Mikey decided to get on board so business in Baisley was booming again. I managed to get a hold of the witness list and one by one they started to disappear. I had left Janelle more than enough money to tide her and the kids over for a few weeks until I got home. There was absolutely no need to give her access to my entire nest egg. I figured with no witnesses and no murder weapons that there would be no case. The only reason I wasn't at home with my family yet was because the court calendar was backlogged, but my date was rapidly approaching and I would once again get to spit in the face of justice and walk out of the courtroom a free man.

The morning of my court date I was like a kid on Christmas morning. I was up at the crack of dawn. The C.O. brought my suit down that Sophia had gotten for me and I was ready to go. As I was escorted to the shuttle bus that would take me to court, hating ass C.O.'s that knew my case told me that they would see me back in a few hours. I just smiled like the cat that ate the canary because I knew different. I knew that in a few hours I would be making love to my wife, and a few hours after that I would be making love to Sophia.

When I arrived at central booking, I was put in a holding cell by myself while I waited for my name to be called. While waiting, I quickly reflected on what landed me in this situation. It was my own stupidity and this was definitely something I would learn from. As usual, I never intended for innocent people to get hurt, especially a kid. Secretly sending the boys family two hundred thousand dollars was added to my list of things to do. It wouldn't bring their kid back, but the kind gesture would make me feel a little better. As far as the chick that was in the car with Bruno, I felt a small feeling of remorse for her, but that's the risk you take when you ride around with a marked man.

"Let's go Outlaw, you're up," the C.O. said as he cracked the cell.

He cuffed me and led me through the long corridor that led to the courtroom.

When I got to the courtroom, I immediately noticed my attorney Jeremy posted up at the defendants table. When I scanned the room, I saw Lorenzo, Shanise, Jo Jo, Sayeed and Sophia sitting with Janelle and the kids. Janelle blew me a kiss, my kids screamed out "hi daddy", and Sophia winked at me as if to say "Don't worry baby, we got this." I was escorted to the defendants' table and the handcuffs were removed.

"Hey Travon, how are you holding up?" Jeremy asked shaking my hand.

"I'm good. I just can't wait for this shit to be over."

"Yeah, well you should be smelling that good old New York pollution in a few hours since from what I hear the states witnesses are no longer with us," he replied winking and nudging me in my arm with his elbow.

"Shut the fuck up Jeremy," I said through gritted teeth.

"All rise, the Honorable Janice M. Reid presiding," the bailiff said as we all stood.

"Be seated," the judge said.

I was lucky as hell to be getting out of here. A few associates of mine had gone up against this bitch and ended up getting hit with major numbers. She was hardnosed and by the book and when she threw the book at you, she threw it hard as fuck.

"Bailiff who do we have on the calendar?" she said.

"Your Honor we have docket number 20120724 the state of New York versus Travon Outlaw. The defendant is charged with three counts of murder in the second degree. The bailiff yelled out.

"Are the parties ready to proceed?" the Judge asked.

The prosecutor stood up.

"Your Honor the state had an air tight case against the defendant; complete with credible and reputable eyewitnesses that put Mr. Outlaw at the scene of this heinous and horrendous crime that claimed the life of an innocent, defenseless child. Each witness named the defendant as the aggressor and the shooter."

"So your answer would be yes then. Correct?"

"Actually your Honor, each of those witnesses have mysteriously turned up murdered, and we believe this to be done at the behest of Mr. Outlaw."

"I object. This is pure speculation," Jeremy yelled.

"Sustained. So the prosecutor is not ready then?"

"Your Honor, the defense moves for an immediate dismissal of all charges. There are no witnesses, no murder weapons, and no need to waste any more of my client or the courts time," Jeremy said as I smiled at Janelle and Sophia who smiled back at me.

"As much as I hate to admit it Mr. Eisenberg, you have a point. With no witnesses and no murder weapon there is no case. I see no other choice but to...."

The prosecutor cut the judge off.

"Your Honor if I may, the state has a surprised witnesses that has very damaging and accurate testimony."

"What fucking surprised witness?" I whispered to Jeremy as my jaw dropped and my knees got weak.

"I object. The defense was not made aware of any surprise witness," Jeremy yelled.

"Yeah well that's why it's called a surprise witness," the prosecutor fired back.

"That is the most unethical crock of bull I have ever heard. Your Honor I ask that this case be thrown out immediately," Jeremy responded.

"Order, order, that's enough," the judge said banging her gavel before continuing.

"Now again, I hate to agree with the defense, but they are right. The state knows the protocol for handing over witness information, both old and new."

"You Honor, you're right. Normal protocol is to make the defense aware of all witnesses, but the way the other witnesses were mysteriously showing up with bullets in the head, it is the states obligation to protect any remaining witness at all cost. Even if it means withholding their name from the defense if we believe the defendant may be responsible for the harm that was done to the other witnesses. Please reference the state of New York versus William Henry 1997. Also at this time the state would like to change the charges from three counts of murder to two counts of murder and one count of attempted murder," he continued handing the bailiff a file to pass to the judge.

My mind raced a million miles a minute as the judge observed the file and Jeremy stood there looking stupid at fifteen hundred dollars an hour.

"Well I stand corrected; it appears that the state did have probable cause to…"

Just then the courtroom door opened and some chick rolled Tiffany in a wheelchair. I couldn't believe my eyes. What the fuck was she doing here? Why was she in a wheelchair? So many scenarios raced through my mind that I had no time to process them all. Somehow I managed to notice that she was as still beautiful as ever. I quickly reminisced about all of the great times we shared together. I was snapped back to reality when we locked eyes and she gave me a look that cut right through me. I noticed the look of surprise and anger on Janelle's face, as Tiffany and her friend sat in the back of the room. I started to sweat profusely as the judge continued.

"As I was saying, I find that the state did have probable cause to withhold the surprise witness."

"This is bullshit!" I yelled out.

"Mr. Outlaw control yourself, or I'll hold you in contempt," the judge stated banging her gavel.

"Can they do this?" I asked Jeremy, who was now reviewing the same file that the judge was.

"Apparently so, who is she and why the hell didn't I know about her?" he responded sounding aggravated.

"That's Tiffany. The little situation I told you about down in Baltimore a few years back."

"Well I thought she was doing like a zillion years in the feds, what the fuck is she doing here Travon?"

"She came for some get back, she came to bury me," I said solemnly.

"Are we ready to proceed?" the judge asked.

"Yes your Honor, we are," the prosecutor responded.

"Okay then, I'll allow this surprised witness, on the condition that you reveal who it is right now and have whoever it is remanded into the witness protection program immediately until these hearings are complete, at which time the witness can stay in the witness protection program and relocate, or opt out. It is solely up to them."

The prosecutor turned to the back of the room and then turned to the judge.

Then out of nowhere I felt a wave of relief take over me as I realized that as bitter as she may have been, Tiffany knew nothing about me. She would be forced to lie and fabricate stories and then Jeremy would shoot her testimony full of holes. I would beat the charges and then make sure Tiffany never got a chance to put me into this position again.

"Your Honor, let the records reflect that Ms. Sophia Garrison has extensive, accurate, and reliable knowledge of the defendants day to day operations including but not limited to drugs, racketeering, falsifying documents, and murders both committed and commissioned including the murders of the states witnesses in this case," the prosecutor responded as he waived Sophia forward.

"You dirty snake ass bitch," Janelle said as Sophia eased passed her.

I was shocked as fuck, and I didn't know what to say do or think. It suddenly seemed like everything was moving in slow motion as I watched my illegitimate counterpart walk passed me and blow a kiss to me, on her way to destroy my life.

"Your Honor. Ms. Garrison is part of Mr. Outlaws legal team and any info that she may or may not have about my client is strictly protected by attorney client privilege."

"Oh well that puts a whole new spin on things. Ms. Garrison you ought to know better, and I warn you that if so much as what Mr. Outlaw eats for breakfast leaks out of your mouth I will have you disbarred and possibly brought up on charges," the judge barked.

"Your Honor if I may address the court. Yes, it is true that at one point and time I did represent Mr. Outlaw, but please let the records show that as of April 7th, 2012 I stopped practicing law and surrendered my license. So I can assure you that my testimony will only include facts from things that took place after this date. All of the drug deals, murders, racketeering, any file that the D.A.'s office has on Mr. Outlaw, I have detailed knowledge of. I have taped confessions of multiple murders including the hit ordered on my younger sister Terri Garrison, who was found shot to death in a Baltimore, Maryland hotel back in 2008 and if that isn't enough to put this bastard away for life, I have possession of the murder weapons used in the murders for which he is currently being charged for in this case," Sophia said shooting me a cold stare.

"Sophia, you sneaky, conniving, snitching bitch. You ain't gotta worry about Travon getting a hold of you. I'm gonna kill you my fucking self," Janelle stood up and screamed, crying in anger.

"Bailiff remove that woman immediately," the judge ordered as Janelle and the kids were escorted out of the courtroom kicking and screaming.

I quickly scanned my brain for all of the information that Sophia had and didn't have. I wanted to blow my own motherfucking head off right then and there as I realized that she knew everything down to the very last detail, but what was this shit about Terri being her sister? I was confused and had no idea what the fuck was going on. I glanced back at Tiffany who appeared to be crying and smiling at the same time.

"Well I guess with that being said, we'll set a trial date for two weeks from today," the judge said interrupting my thoughts.

"In light of the new evidence does the defendant wish to change his plea at this time?"

"A moment to confer with my client your Honor?" Jeremy asked.

"Make it quick. This circus has already taken up enough of the courts time."

"Okay Travon. Give it to me straight. How much does that bitch Sophia really know?"

"Everything," I responded in disgust.

"Fuck dude. How could you be so stupid?"

"Whoa. Who the fuck you calling stupid? She's my attorney, or at least I thought she was. Now watch your motherfucking mouth before I make them add another charge to my docket," I snapped.

"Look. All I'm saying is that I bet I don't know everything she knows, and I have been representing you ever since you were a snotty nosed kid getting busted with nickel bags of weed. You were thinking with your dick, and now you're fucked. No pun intended."

"Okay Jeremy. You can give me the history lesson later. What do you suggest I do?"

"Well the drug murders they can probably give two shits about you can probably claim self defense on that one, but you killed a ten-year old white boy during the course of a drug related shoot out. They will probably seek the death penalty; however there has not been a court sanctioned execution in the state of New York since 1976, so you're good as far as that goes, and up until now your record is squeaky clean. If we plead out I can shoot for twenty, with good behavior you'll be out in twelve years tops, maybe even less."

"Give it to me straight. Do we have any chance of beating this?"

"Travon, if I said yes I would just be robbing you blind."

"Alright then. Make the deal. I still have an ace in the hole that I have been holding for just such an occasion."

"You're the boss. Your Honor may we approach the bench?"

THE RUNDOWN

Soon after the attorney's approached the bench, we were asked to clear the courtroom. I was in shock and had no idea what was going on. In the weeks that I had been in the hospital, I made sure Monica had no way to contact or visit me because I was registered in the hospital under the alias name listed on the drivers license that was found in my purse the day I was shot. I could feel myself losing my mind again, and that feeling felt all too familiar, so I called the only person that I had left on this earth and that was Michelle. When I told her what went down she was on the next thing smoking to New York. Once I was cleared to leave the hospital Michelle checked me into the Ritz Carlton under another one of the alias names that she had drawn up for me. She suggested we immediately head back to Baltimore, and as much as I knew she was right, I just couldn't leave until I saw this thing through with Travon. And the fact that the motherfucker shot me and almost killed me only added fuel to the fire. So I insisted on staying until I saw what happened with his case. The case was so high profiled that I learned through the media when his court date was, and I ordered Michelle to roll my ass down to the courthouse. I never expected to see or hear what I did.

What was Sophia doing here? What the fuck was this shit about her representing Travon? I definitely needed answers and I wasn't leaving until I got them. When we got into the hallway Monica came running up.

"Oh shit am I too late? Did I miss it? Oh my god. Tiffany are you okay? Where have you been?" she asked out of breath.

I mustered up enough energy to painfully lift myself from my wheelchair and punch that bitch in the face. When she fell to the ground I jumped on her attempting to beat the shit out of her.

"Whoop that bitches ass," Michelle screamed as others in the hallway called for help.

"I should fucking kill you bitch," I yelled as every swing of my arms sent excruciating pain through my body.

A few court officers came running over and broke up the fight.

"What the fuck is wrong with you Tiffany? Calm the fuck down," Monica said attempting to fix her hair and clothes.

"Bitch ain't no where you can run to or move to that will keep me from digging in your ass."

"Tiffany calm down and listen to me."

"Fuck that bitch Tiff. I told you she was a shady bitch from the jump," Michelle said.

"Now listen here Michelle. I'm holding back on Tiffany because she's like my sister, but you on the other hand ain't shit to me, and I ain't never liked you anyway so I don't have no problem splitting your shit to the white meat. You feel me hoe?"

"Whatever bitch."

"Okay ladies. That's enough. Please clear the hallway," one of the court officers demanded.

As we started to leave Travon was being escorted out in handcuffs. I rolled my eyes and turned my head.

"Let's go Michelle."

"Tiffany wait," he called out.

"Let's go Mr. Outlaw. The court officer ordered.

"No hold up. It's cool, let the motherfucker speak," I said.

"You got one minute," the officer said looking at his watch.

"Tiffany, I never had a chance to apologize for what I did. You have to know how sorry I am for everything. I never meant to hurt you. What I did to you was fucked up on so many levels and not a day went by that I didn't think about it. That's why I had that bitch get you out and that's the part that hurts baby. I go out of my way to get you out of prison and then you do me like this? At least I tried to fix what I fucked up," he admitted with tears in his eyes.

"Do you like what Travon? This is my first time hearing about any of this, and I had nothing to do with it, but I wish I did motherfucker."

Just then Sophia came out escorted by a court officer. She noticed that something had just went down and rushed over to Monica.

"Oh my god Monica, are you okay?" she said before she and Monica engaged in a long passionate kiss as the rest of us looked on. I was totally fucked up now.

"Baby is it over?" Monica asked.

"Almost baby, almost," Sophia responded.

"Wow. So it was you two hoes. You know, if my hands were free I'd applaud you both." Travon said smiling.

"Yeah well the day that you had somebody harm my little sister Terri, you gained an enemy for life motherfucker, accident or no accident," Sophia spat.

"Wow. So you lay in my bed for three fucking years pretending you cared, pretending to love me, but the whole time you were just soaking up info huh? You conveniently stopped practicing law and surrendered your license the day after we got Tiffany out of jail, well played bitch, well played," Travon said.

"Yeah nigga you cost my sister her life too. You played the shit out of Tiffany and you already know how the Stiletto Diva's rock, so we did the same exact shit to you. How does it feel motherfucker?" Monica jumped in.

Travon started laughing hysterically.

"You sure are laughing pretty hard for somebody who's about to do an asshole full of time," Sophia said.

"Come on now Ma, you have been with me damn near everyday for the last three years. You know how powerful I am in this city and you know I got money longer than train smoke so the New York penal system ain't got shit on me. I got friends in places I ain't even tell you about, so I'll be seeing ya'll bitches a lot sooner than ya'll think. When I do, it ain't gonna be pretty," he responded smiling.

"I hope you're going to report that you witnessed these threats," I yelled to the court officers.

"Oh Gary here? He ain't heard shit. We play ball together every Saturday, and if you know what's good for you Officer Vasquez you ain't see shit either. So like I said, I'll be seeing ya'll real soon. By the way Tiffany, why are you in a wheel chair?"

"Because you shot me motherfucker!"

"What?"

"I was in the car with Bruno Travon. So once again you have fucked my life up."

"What? Why the fuck was you in the car with him? Tiff baby I had no idea."

"Travon, look at me. Does it look like it matters anymore? Your apologies for ruining my life are starting to sound like you are copying and pasting a fucking Facebook status. I hope you rot in hell?

"What! Well don't hold your breath waiting for that. Let's go Gary," he said as he winked at me.

And with that being said, Travon was lead away.

"Don't worry ya'll. This fight is far from over," Sophia stated.

"Come on Ms. Garrison. We'd better get you out of here," Officer Vasquez said.

I was so confused. I definitely needed answers to what was going on.

NOW IT ALL MAKES SENSE

I reluctantly agreed that Monica, Michelle, and I would grab a bite to eat at the diner across the street from the courthouse. I figured that I would stay close since at this point I still wasn't fucking with Monica. It's a good thing I had Michelle come down a few weeks ago, she helped nurse me back to health. You see the day of the shooting a few of Travon's stray bullets hit me in the stomach and ruptured my spleen, and punctured both of my lungs. It was a good thing that the shootout took place in Manhattan because the paramedics were at the scene in seconds and they were able to resuscitate me. It would be a long time before I was back to a hundred percent, but I thanked God that I was alive. We sat down at a table and immediately waived off the waitress that was on her way.

"Okay Monica, you got ten minutes. What the fuck is going on?" I asked.

"Damn. Where do I start?"

"Try the fucking beginning," Michelle said sarcastically.

"You mind your fucking business hoe. If it wasn't for you, my girl wouldn't be in this mess."

"You got a lot of nerve. As dirty as you did your so called friend, bitch you need your ass whopped bloody," Michelle screamed.

"Excuse me ladies, I am going to have to ask you to keep your voices down," a passing waitress said.

"Talk Monica," I said, getting aggravated again.

"I'm trying to. Look, shortly after you got booked for all that bullshit back in B-More. I was down at the Pink Lizard; you know the lesbian bar down on Baltimore Street. Well anyway, I was in the bathroom washing my hands, and there was Sophia at the sink next to me doing the same thing. I knew she looked familiar, but I couldn't place the face. In any event I wanted to get to know her, so I introduced myself and invited her back over to my table. She accepted and we were back at the table drinking and getting to know each other, then I asked her where she was from and she said New York, but she came to B-More to handle some affairs for her half sister who had been killed. So naturally because I know every damn body in B-more, I asked who her sister was and I'll be damned if she didn't say Terri Franklin."

"Our Terri Franklin?" I asked perplexed.

"Yes our Terri Franklin."

"But Terri ain't have no sister."

"Girl, Terri crazy ass had a sister and a daughter that she ain't never tell us about. That's where I recognized Sophia from. I saw her briefly at Terri's funeral. She ducked in and out because she couldn't take it."

"What? A daughter, that's not possible."

"I'll be damned if it ain't. It turns out that she had a four-year-old daughter that her aunt kept for her since birth. It seems that Terri didn't want no kids because she didn't want to be tied down and she would rather run the streets."

"Are you fucking serious?"

"Wait. I'm not done. Sophia was in town handling some legal business concerning Terri's daughter. She said that her and Terri had just recently become close, and that they began talking almost every night. Sophia knew all about us and everything we did. She didn't approve of our lifestyle and was trying to convince Terri to take the baby and move to New York."

"I can't believe what I'm hearing. In the courtroom she yelled about Travon killing Terri. What the fuck was that about?"

"Well apparently Terri was out and about doing her solo thing one night trying to get some bread. She was asked to run some coke up to Georgetown. As it turns out, the run was for Travon, and you know Terri and her greedy ass, God bless her, she was attempting to black mail Travon. She threatened to tell you what type of shit he was into. He damn near begged her not to say anything, so she knew he would do anything to keep that info from you. So the night she was at the hotel, she called Sophia and told her what her plans were. She told Sophia that Travon had agreed to pay her, and he was sending someone over to pay her off. Terri never said how much she hit Travon up for, but she said it was more than enough for her and the baby to relocate and be comfortable for a while. She also told Sophia that she planned on fucking Travon over and telling you anyway. He must have known that, so he sent D-Boy over there to rough Terri up, and according to Travon, Terri put up a fight so the D-Boy popped her."

"Oh my God. So Travon was behind Terri's death?"

"Yes he was. When that punk nigga Gerard got to the hotel room, Terri was already dead."

"I'm starting to feel light headed."

"Waitress can we have some water please?" Michelle asked.

"Keep going Monica. I need to hear all of this once and for all," I said.

"Well Sophia had mentioned that she would do anything to get back at Travon. So I told her I knew exactly who he was and what he had done to you. I told her that I wanted to pay his bitch ass back too. After having so much in common and obviously being attracted to one another we hit it off great and started alternating weekend visits between B-more and New York, and before I knew it we were in love."

"Hold up. Hold the fuck up. The great and powerful Monica Dean in love?" I joked.

"Bitch shut the fuck up and listen. Anyway Sophia and me were in bed one night and I came up with a plan to get that motherfucker Travon back. Since Travon was a sucker for dime chicks, and Sophia was one of the baddest bitches I had ever seen, I figured that we would plant her in his life and totally fuck it up from the inside out. We collectively did our homework and found out as much stuff about him as we could. His likes, dislikes, hangouts, and day-to-day operations. Surprisingly that was the hard part;

the easy part was having Sophia walk into his life and totally fuck his head up, the way he fucked yours up. The original plan was just for Sophia to get close enough for him to confess to her what he had done. She would then take that information to her friends in the D.A. office. But Travon was too smart for that. He was tight lipped for months, and we were getting nowhere. We were just about to throw in the towel, but when Sophia came up with the idea to lie about her and her family's background, he started to open up almost immediately. Then when she told him that she could help him out because she had friends in the D.A.'s office, he bought the act hook, line, and sinker. Then he did something to make our job a hell of a lot easier."

"What did he do?" I asked, hanging onto her every word.

"He retained Sophia as his attorney. Once he did that, she started pouring it on extra thick. The nigga Travon was really feeling her. I mean he was feeling her, like he was feeling you. Then one day he spilled his guts about damn near everything he ever did."

"Okay, but why would he risk telling her about all of his dirt?" Michelle asked.

"That nigga is a lot of things but he ain't no dummy. He hid behind attorney/client privilege."

"What's that?" I asked.

"Basically what it means is that you can tell your attorney anything in the world and by law they can't legally use it against you or tell anyone for that matter. Just like a priest or a shrink. In that pussy's defense, all of that shit was weighing heavy on him. He couldn't wait to get that shit off his chest. It was actually his idea to get you out, " Monica explained.

"So if that whole attorney/client thing is true, then how is Sophia turning states evidence on him."

"Sophia knew that she was in deep and that shit was going to get thick, so the day after you were released, she gave up her license to practice law. Obviously she never told Travon, and he just kept running his dumb ass mouth. Periodically she would go to the D.A.'s office with information but apparently it was considered hearsay and wasn't good enough. It wasn't until the day you got shot that she actually had enough to give them. They needed to catch him red handed on something recent, in order to open cases on the old shit."

"Damn that was a smart ass plan, but how come you kept it from me? Why didn't you just tell me?" I asked.

"That was Sophia's call. She didn't think you would be able to keep your cool. She said something about you still possible having feelings for this nigga when she first came to see you. I should smack your ass for that, but at the end of the day, she didn't want to risk you fucking up her plans to get Travon back and neither one of us wanted you getting hurt."

"Damn ya'll bitches really are ruthless. All them stories Tiff told me about ya'll in the Feds was true huh?" Michelle asked just as shocked as I was at the story.

"You already know. The Stiletto Diva's take care of their own," Monica replied.

"Wow. I can't believe you and Sophia put it down like that," I said with tears of joy in my eyes.

"Come on now. You know there is nothing in this world I wouldn't do for you."

"Damn Monica. I am so sorry I doubted your friendship and loyalty. I'm sorry I jumped on you too."

"It ain't about shit. I know shit must have looked really crazy and I wanted to tell you so bad but I promised my baby that I wouldn't say a word. As far as you jumping on me, don't sweat it. When you are all healed up we are going to the gym and putting the gloves on," Monica joked.

"Okay you can get that. So now what?"

"We wait."

"Wait for what?"

"We just wait."

OUT OF THE FRYING PAN

My ace in the hole managed to come through for me. I had a connection in the State Department that I vowed to only use in case of an emergency. If you're wondering how a drug dealer from South Jamaica, Queens had a connection in the State Department, the answer is simple; everybody does some type of drug, you just have to find the right people that need your services. My connection assured me that if I kept his name a secret he would make sure the charges were reduced to two counts of involuntary manslaughter and one charge of reckless assault and if I plead out I would only be looking at five years max, home in two with good behavior. So that's what I did. The D.A.'s office tried their best to squeeze my team, but they all stood their ground just as I knew that they would. Everything was going fine. Lorenzo was handling business in my absence and there were no issues at all. I had allowed Janelle access to enough money to last her and the kids about three years. I figured with that and the weekly allowance that Lorenzo was dropping off to her there would be no reason to give her access to all of my money. Wife or no wife, that's only something you do in case of emergency.

Over the next few months I had received regular visits from Janelle and the kids, as well as Lorenzo and the crew. Shanise was a trip, as hard as she was on the outside she was soft as baby shit on the inside. There was never a visit where she didn't break down crying. I love that girl on many different levels. Truth be told, as long as I had breath in my body Shanise would always be taken care of. My thoughts were interrupted by a C.O. walking the tier.

"Outlaw you got mail," he said as he handed me a large stack of envelopes.

"Good looking my dude," I said as I shuffled threw mad envelopes.

I received so much mail on a daily basis that I never had time to read them all at once. So I just rifled through them to see who was showing me love and I would get to reading them later. I was shuffling through the mail when I saw an envelope that came for the Maryland State Attorney's Office. I suddenly felt a large lump in my throat and my hands suddenly began to shake as I ripped the envelope open. As my eyes scanned the letter, I wasn't even passed the third line when my heart started beating through my chest. My worst fears had been confirmed. The state of Maryland had re-opened their case that they had against Tiffany, but and since I got her off the hook, I was now the target. That bitch Sophia had done it again. This could not have come from anyone but her. I used every resource I had to find that bitch and have her buried, once she shitted on me the first time, but she was nowhere to be found. She had checked herself out of the Witness Protection Program and was off on her own somewhere. Once again, she held my life in her hands, and unlike New York, I had absolutely no connections in Baltimore. I was going to have to ride this one out.

Over the next few months, Jeremy and I had been fighting the Baltimore case from my New York jail cell. Unfortunately we were getting our asses kicked. I had simply given Sophia too many details about my dealings in Baltimore. In the essence of saving the taxpayers money, I was offered a plea bargain. The D.A. offered a deal of twenty-five to life if I plead guilty to the charges of murder, conspiracy to commit murder, and interstate drug trafficking. If I took it to trial and lost, I would be facing life without the possibility of parole. The way I saw it, I was only twenty-eight. I figured even with a twenty-five to life sentence to start immediately after my New York sentence, I would still be home in my early to mid fifties. Shit, that's still young enough to take back what's rightfully mines in these streets. I immediately called Janelle, gave her the news and told her to make sure she was here on the next visit so I could give her a list of instructions. This new indictment changed the dynamics of a lot of things.

A few days later Janelle showed up to the visit without the kids just like I had told her to. I could see the look of hurt, fear and anger in her eyes.

"Hey baby. You look good," I said trying to lighten the mood.

"Cut the shit Travon. This is no time for jokes. What are we going to do?"

"Baby, have I ever let you down? Now things are going to be okay. Whatever time I have to do will go by fast, trust me."

"Twenty-five years Travon. How am I supposed to live without my other half for twenty-five years baby? And what about the boys? What are they going to do without a father?" she whispered as tears streamed down her face.

"Baby listen, remember from day one we talked about the possibility of this day coming. I told you what the plan of action was if I ever had to go away for an extended amount of time. I told you how to conduct yourself in my absence."

"Yes I know we talked about it Travon, but that was years ago and with everything going so smoothly I never imagined this day coming. I can't do this without you Travon. I just can't, you have to come home baby."

"Listen to me. You can do it and you will do it. Now you're stronger than this. Pull yourself together because this is no time for you to fall apart. Now I'm not trying to put any pressure on you but if you can't stick with the plan then we are not going to survive this ordeal. Now the fun and games are over. We had a good run that lasted well over ten years, but I fucked up so it's time to put our plan into action."

"Okay Travon. Give it to me again baby. I'm sorry. I'll be strong. I got your back baby."

"Alright listen. You see how I have been conducting myself with Lorenzo and the crew. You conduct yourself the exact same way. I've had Jeremy put the club, houses, and cars all in your name. You carry on my name and represent me with your head held high, until I come home. It's simple you do everything that you know I would do, and you do nothing that you know I wouldn't do you hear me?" I asked as I now had her full attention and she hung in every word.

"Yes baby, I hear you. But what if Lorenzo and them don't listen to me?"

"They will listen to you, because I have had this same conversation with each of them before. I never wanted this day to come, but I have always planned for it."

"Okay Tray, I got you baby, is there anything else?"

"Yeah, you are to never miss a visit or a phone call, even when they move me upstate and then to Maryland. I need to see you every week and I will see you every week, do you understand me?"

"Of course Travon, that goes without saying."

"Good, and there is one more thing."

"What is it?"

"In case of an emergency, meaning in case I don't make it out of here, I want to make sure you and the kids are set for life."

"Wait. Stop. I don't want to hear this Travon. You will make it out of here; nothing is going to happen to you. Don't talk like that," she said crying harder.

"Shhh. Listen to me. My plan is to make it out of here, but we have to account for the possibility that anything can happen. That's all I'm doing baby, I'm accounting for the possibility."

"What. What is it Travon?"

"Okay you know those three watches in my jewelry closet that you always complain about?"

"The ones with the wrong times on them?

"Yeah."

"What about them? Is that what you are leaving your wife and kids, three broke ass watches?" She said, attempting to joke through the heavy downpour of tears.

"No smart ass. The times on those watches from left to right are the combination to a safe I have in the basement."

"What safe in the basement? I never knew about a safe in the basement."

"Yeah I know you didn't. Anyway the safe is under the couch. I had it built into the floor when you were in Vegas a few years back. You will have to move the couch and then cut away the carpet in order to get to the safe."

"Damn Mr. Secretive."

"Be quiet. I kept it from you for your own good. Now inside that safe is the key to a safety deposit box. Inside that safety deposit box is the whole kit and caboodle. Everything I am worth, everything we are worth is in that box."

"Holy shit. How much is in there Travon?"

"A little over thirty eight million dollars."

"THIRTY EIGHT MILLION DOLLARS?" She yelled louder than she meant to.

"Shut the fuck up Janelle. Damn, why don't you just let everybody know?"

"I'm sorry baby, I'm just in shock. I mean I knew we were living good, but I had no idea we were sitting on that kind of paper."

"Yeah well, everything ain't for you to know. Now that money is only to be touched if something should ever happen to me. There is more than enough money coming to you so you should never have to touch that money. You understand me?"

"Yes Travon, I understand."

"Now like I said, nothing changes. We are going to get through this and when I get home we are taking the kids and moving far away. Maybe London or some other crazy place like that. I'm done with this life baby."

"Oh Travon I would love that. When you come home, London it is. There is nothing left for us here. Let's take the kids and go."

"Okay baby. Even though they won't be kids anymore we will still be a happy family. I am sorry for putting you through all of this."

"Look baby. Stop apologizing. I knew what I signed on for when I met you. I knew all the risks. I just prayed this day would never come. Don't sweat it my King, when you come home everything will still be all good. Your Queen will rule in your absence."

"That's what I'm talking about baby. That's why I put that ten karat pink diamond on your finger and gave you my last name."

"Yup and two handsome sons."

"Okay Outlaw, that's your time," A C.O. shouted.

"Well look baby, I have to go. You remember everything I told you and everything I ever taught you. Keep repping your King in true fashion. You hear me."

"No doubt baby. I'll be up with the boys next week. They miss you."

"I love ya'll and I miss ya'll too. Oh and one more thing baby."

"What's that Tray?"

"If you even think about burning me, I don't care if you did give life to our kids, there will be no where on this earth you can hide. You already know what I'm capable of."

"Wow. I can't believe you just said that to me, you should know better but I forgive you baby."

"Good. I'll see you next week, but I will call you every day. I love you."

"I love you more Travon."

I blew her a kiss and headed back to my cell. It was time to get adjusted to my new life.

LIFE AFTER DEATH

Monica, Michelle and I had been back in Baltimore for awhile now. I was still recovering and still soaking in everything that had taken place in New York. I'm not quite sure if what happened would ever make sense to me. Today though, there was another mystery on my mind. Monica had dragged me to the airport and would not give me a reason why, it wasn't until we got to the airport that I found out we were going to Miami.

"Okay Monica, what the hell is this Miami trip all about?"

"You need a vacation. A real vacation, one that doesn't involve your silly ass getting shot."

"Ha ha, very funny bitch. Well you better be glad you're footing the bill or else my happy shot up ass would be right the fuck at the crib."

"Yeah I know. Come on with your cheap ass."

I just laughed as we boarded our first class flight to Miami. During the flight Monica fell asleep instantly. She was apparently still hung over from hanging out the night before. Me on the other hand, I had stayed home. I was in no mood to party and was not sure that I would be anytime soon. During the flight I had nothing but time to reflect on everything that had taken place and I asked myself. Now that it was over, was it all worth it? Travon was in jail, and I would walk with a limp forever. So in the end, what did I really accomplish? It just seems like my life fell completely apart after my Mom and Dad passed away. I wonder if they are disappointed in me and the choices I made, or if they know that I was just misguided in their absence. All of this thinking was making my head hurt. I asked the stewardess for an aspirin and a pillow and drifted off to sleep.

"*Ladies and Gentlemen we are now arriving in sunny Miami, Florida. The weather is a beautiful eighty two degrees. Please wait for the seatbelt sign to be turned off before exiting the aircraft. Enjoy your stay in Miami, and we thank you for flying with us.*"

The announcement had awakened Monica and me up simultaneously. We stretched, fixed our clothes, grabbed our overhead luggage and exited the plane. Being back in Miami was bitter sweet for me. The first, last and only time I had ever been here was with Travon. Which was subsequently the same weekend that he had Terri killed. My stomach started to do cartwheels and my knees got weak as we stepped out into the fresh Miami air. Monica hailed a cab and directed him to take us to the Shore Club hotel. When we got to the hotel we tipped the driver, checked in, gave the porter our luggage and headed up to our suite. When we got to the suite I immediately plopped down on the couch.

"Ouch. Damn I keep forgetting I can't be just doing that shit anymore," I said wincing as I grabbed my stomach where I had been shot."

"Bitch if you sit your little happy ass still, you won't have those problems. The doctor said it's going to be tender for a very long time. You don't even use the cane he gave you."

"Um I am too damn sexy to be walking with a cane. I will take my chances with the sexy limp thank you very much."

"You know you about a simple bitch. I'm about to take a shower and change into something more Miami like."

"Okay you go ahead. I'm going to relax right here and wait for you."

"You don't have to wait for me. There is a shower in your room too Tiff."

"Girl I am not getting changed. We don't even know what we're doing yet. Just go ahead and get showered. I wanna rest up for a few more minutes anyway."

"Okay suit yourself. When the porter brings the bags up give him a nice tip, he was a cutie," she replied as she grabbed her Loui bag and headed towards her room.

"Okay I got you, and yeah he was a cutie with his young self."

"Maybe we can get him up here for a threesome."

"Shut up Monica," I said laughing as she shut the door and started running the shower water.

Monica liked taking long hot showers so I knew I had at least twenty minutes to relax before she attempted to drag me all over South Beach. I turned on the T.V. and was flipping through the channels. I caught a glimpse of the Real Housewives of Atlanta, so I kept it on that channel to catch up on what I had missed. I was really into the show when there was a knock at the door. I reached in my purse and grabbed a twenty-dollar bill to give the cute young porter. I opened the door and almost fainted from my knees buckling as I was staring Travon's wife in the face.

My survival instincts kicked in and although it hurt like hell, I jumped on her and immediately began fighting with every ounce of energy I had. I was screaming for Monica, but she couldn't hear me over the shower water. The pain from my wounds caused a handicap for me as Travon's wife started to get the best of me. I knew why she was here; I just didn't know how she knew where I was. In any event, her killing me wasn't going to be easy. I would fight with every bone in my body to stay alive but it was truly becoming a task. I was losing the wrestling match, as Travon's wife rolled me over and was now on top of me. I screamed for dear life as she reached into her Gucci clutch that had fallen to the floor besides us. I closed my eyes and said a quick prayer, I waited for the shot but it never came. Instead I was slapped across the face.

"What the fuck is wrong with you? Here you crazy bitch," Travon's wife said upset and out of breath.

I opened my eyes and saw an envelope in her hand.

"What the fuck is that?" I responded equally out of breath.

"It's a check for over six million dollars bitch. Now take it before I change my fucking mind."

"Hey Tiff did they bring our bags up yet? What the fuck? Yo get the fuck off of her," Monica yelled walking in and catching Travon's wife sitting on top of me, as she grabbed her and threw her to the ground.

"Monica chill the fuck out. She attacked me first," Travon's wife explained.

"You okay Tiff?" Monica asked helping me up off the floor.

"I'll be okay, but once again can somebody tell me what the fuck is going on?"

"It's simple, a few years back Sophia and I found somebody who hated Travon just as much as the rest of us did. So we cut a deal with her."

"What? What deal? What are you talking about?"

"Travon has been spoon feeding me since we have been together. He always controlled every financial move I made. For years I wanted to leave him, but I knew I would get nothing in a divorce because all of his damn money is dirty. I hated him for controlling my life, I hated him for cheating on me for years, and believe it or not I hated him for what he did to you. I just couldn't leave because I needed him for stability. So I stuck around and played my role. I knew that Travon had a nest egg somewhere, and I knew the only way I would ever get access to it was if he felt he had no choice but to give it to me. The only way that would happen would be if he got his ass jammed up like he is now. So when Monica and Sophia approached me a few years back and they told me about this plan I was like fuck it. I had nothing to lose, and everything to gain. I was all in from day one. It took long as hell, but it worked. So that's why I'm here to give you your cut. Travon was sitting on thirty eight million. Fifty percent is for the kids and me, and the rest is for ya'll to split three ways. Which comes out to a little bit over six million dollars apiece for you, Monica, and Sophia.

The deal was also contingent on the fact that you each open up a trust fund for Terri's daughter and contribute half a million apiece," Travon's wife explained.

"So wait a minute. How did you and Sophia know you could trust her? What was to stop her from just running off with all the money?" I asked.

"Pure woman's intuition. You never fuck with a scorned woman," Monica responded smiling.

"Wow. I can't believe it. Six million dollars and change and it's all mines? Wait. Is this check gonna bounce?" I asked.

"Nope. Sophia was on top of that. These are cashier's checks," Monica said getting her own check out of the girl's purse.

"Speaking of Sophia. Where is she?" I asked.

"She's downstairs waiting, and we better hurry up or we're going to miss the boat," Travon's wife answered.

"What damn boat?"

"We're going to the Bahamas to celebrate," Monica responded.

"What? Wait. I'm not dressed for that," I said excitedly.

"Bitch you are a millionaire now. Shop when we get there," Monica said laughing.

"Okay fuck it then. Let's be out," I said grinning like a big kid.

I grabbed my purse and travel bag and turned to Travon's wife.

"Hello, my name is Tiffany, nice to meet you."

"Hi Tiffany. I'm Janelle," she said shaking my hand.

INTO THE FIRE

I was in my cell awaiting my weekly visit from Janelle. I will admit that it took a lot for me to give her that safety deposit box info, but nothing changed when I gave it to her. She still sent mail, kept money on my books and made her weekly visits with a smile on her face. I spoke to Lorenzo and Shanise, and they both said she was handling business accordingly and that I had taught her well. I was reading a magazine waiting for my name to be called and it seemed like it was taking forever. I looked at the clock and saw that visiting hour had started eight minutes ago. It was not like Janelle to be late; maybe she got caught in traffic or something I tried to rationalize with myself. The clock kept ticking and my name never got called for a visit. I tried to call her, only to find out the bitch put a block on the phone. Now there was no more reason to speculate. Janelle had burned me, after I warned her not too. My next call was to Lorenzo.

"*Yo what's good Gee?*" he asked as he answered the phone.

"A Yo. Have you seen Janelle today?"

"*Nah. She ain't even come see me this morning for her weekly envelope. I ain't think nothing of it though. I just figured*

277

she was running late. I was actually on my way to your crib to drop it off to her."

"How far are you from the crib?"

"Shit I'm pulling up on your block right now."

"When she answers the door, put that bitch on the phone son."

"Um, Boss I don't think she's going to answer the door."

"Why the fuck not?"

"Because there is a for sale sign out front. The crib is empty."

"FUCK! You remember the plan if this was to happen right?"

"Yup. I know it like the back of my hand," he reassured me.

"Find her, and make her miss me," I said as I slammed the phone down repeatedly.

I felt myself getting light headed as I walked back to my cell. Other inmates were speaking to me as I passed, but I had no idea what they were saying. The bitch had burned me, and my only hope now was that Lorenzo found her before she got ghost with all of my money. His instructions were to find her, take care of her and give the kids to Shanise until I came home. That was the contingency plan that I never wanted to implement, but now it was necessary. Janelle deserved everything that was about to come her way. When I got back to my cell I laid down and just stared at the ceiling. I know that praying to God that Lorenzo found Janelle was probably wrong, but I did it anyway. I was lost in my own thoughts when a female C.O. tapped on the cell bars with her nightstick.

"Outlaw you got mail," she said as she handed me an envelope.

I sat up and took it from her. There was no letter inside the envelope. Just a necklace with what appeared to be a diamond encrusted high heel shoe pendant hanging from it. I was lost.

"Where did this come from? Who are you? I ain't seen you around here before?"

"I'm a transfer from Cumberland Federal Prison in Maryland. My name is Washington, and Tiffany sends her love motherfucker."

Before I could process what she said, she had squirted some type of liquid all over me, lit a match and tossed it on me.

REDEMPTION

Know I know ya'll didn't think I was just going to let Sophia, Janelle, and Monica have all the fun with Travon's bitch ass did you? There is nothing worse than a woman's scorn, especially a rich woman. So when I heard that Washington was transferred to the same prison that Travon was in, I offered her half a million to pay him a little visit for me and surprisingly she jumped at the opportunity with no hesitation. I don't know if it was the money, or the fact that she just had genuine love for me. Maybe it was both, but for me it was never about the money, that was an unexpected bonus. Truth be told I would have given Washington all of my money if she would have asked for it. I was more concerned with being able to sleep at night, and moving on with my life, and the only way that was going to happen was with me dealing with Travon once and for all. So the fact that I was released from prison almost a year ago meant nothing.....now I was truly free.

www.ingramcontent.com/pod-product-compliance
Lightning Source LLC
Chambersburg PA
CBHW072323280626
47159CB00027B/872